KELPIE BLUE

Out of Underhill, Book One

Mell Eight

A NineStar Press Publication

www.ninestarpress.com

Kelpie Blue

Printed in the USA

ISBN: 978-1-64890-180-5

NineStar Edition, December, 2020
Originally Published in March 2018

Also available in eBook, ISBN: 978-1-64890-179-9

WARNING:

This book contains sexual content, which may only be suitable for mature readers, and depiction of abduction/kidnapping.

When a beautiful blue horse asks Rin to go for a swim, Rin doesn't realize how much his life is about to change. Blue is unlike anyone else Rin has ever met, and the magic of the fae, and of this particular kelpie, is wondrous, but deadly. Rin learns too late he might be in for a swim he won't survive.

A Promise and a Warning

Written By: Unknown

Faery dust and the rolling greens
A life of love, a love of thrills
We the people from under the hills
Offer the sweetest of dreams

Ware, you be and you will live
For the wee folk take all
Then laugh, happy as you fall
And our pains we never forgive

Of Underhill and overstone
Lakes and rivers that always flow
Skies above and the caverns below
The faery court rules by blood and bone

Faery dust and the rolling greens
Devious, cruel, and oh so sweet
You should hope we never do meet
Above, below, and always unseen

Tell me, how good is your luck tonight?

Chapter One

Mama was a cowboy. Okay, technically she was a cowgirl, but that's beside the point. She grew up in the South, with a capital S. Her childhood was full of Bible-thumping, cattle, and hay. There wasn't much room for school, especially since she was a girl. Her job was to help around the farmhouse, milk the cows, get married, and have a brood of kids who would grow up to work the farm too.

But, like I said, Mama was a cowboy. She wore pants and rode horses. She skipped church to nurse a sick calf. She could milk the damned cows, cook, and clean, but she didn't have to like it. Her parents tried to set her straight, but Mama would sneak out to play with the colts in the paddock instead of sewing with her girlfriends. She would go out to the movies or even drive to a club in the neighboring city with friends who had never heard that girls only ever wore full skirts.

There were girls like Mama who cropped up in farm families from time to time, and the general consensus was she'd grow out of it soon. It was childhood rebellion, and it would fade.

Then I appeared. No, not like magic—poof, suddenly there was a baby in Mama's arms. At first, her Sunday dresses were a bit too tight, and then her jeans wouldn't button. Babies were fine in the South, so long as there was a husband to go along with them. Mama didn't even have a man offering to court her, let alone a boyfriend or a fiancé. She had met a drifter, someone who came with the cows from Texas and was gone a few days later. There were men who thought Mama was beautiful despite her prickly personality and the baby growing inside, and they offered for her hand, thinking she couldn't say no. Her parents were relieved—they could cover up the baby mistake with a quick wedding—but Mama always said no.

Her parents turned her out. Mama said she thought they were planning to set up a wedding anyway, so when she crawled back to them in desperation, they could tuck her firmly under their thumbs and end her rebellion forever. Instead, Mama hopped on the first train heading north and never looked back.

She worked as a waitress, saving every dime, until labor pains made her supervisor call an ambulance.

Her tips were huge that day, enough that when she got out of the hospital, she could finally afford to buy an old farm left unoccupied for the last decade. The forest on part of the land was haunted, the locals told her, and people kept disappearing. No one would buy it; the bank practically gave it away to Mama for free.

I was a quiet baby, so her supervisor let her keep me behind the counter when she returned to work. Her money mostly went to diapers, but every once in a while she'd call in a contractor. The barn got fixed up first. The fences around the massive home paddock were next. She put a new roof on the farmhouse and replaced some rotting wood around the foundation. Eventually, she bought two retired racehorses.

The horses themselves weren't anything special. They hadn't won stakes races, and their thoroughbred pedigree wasn't anything to laud, but they were good-looking horses all the same. Mama knew horses, and when she got some foals out of them, she taught the babies how to run.

Mama's horses won stakes races. She cut her hours at the restaurant to spend more time training her colts and fillies. She bought more pedigree horses and built a second paddock so the stud stallions wouldn't fight over their mares. She was eventually able to build a third paddock solely for training.

I was ten years old at that point, and Mama had an amazing reputation as a trainer and breeder.

Owners would bring their thoroughbreds to her for training. She quit her job at the restaurant and built a second barn with an indoor training ring. The barn was so large she could run the horses inside in bad weather. I was glad because it meant I didn't have to clear the snow from the paddocks in the winter.

I was almost fourteen when it all ended. We were driving home from the racetrack with two horses in the trailer behind our truck. Mama never saw the drunk driver who hit us. He came whipping around a curve in the road, well over the double yellow line. When I woke up, I was in the hospital. Mama was in the bed next to me.

The weight of the horses in the trailer had saved our lives. We hadn't gone over the ridge, and our car hadn't flipped because the trailer had prevented it. Mama had broken ribs and a broken hip. I had severe compound fractures in my legs. The drunk driver was dead.

I turned fourteen in the hospital. Mama traveled between the farm and the hospital for weeks after she was released. It was almost a year before she could properly sit a horse, but she never had the strength in her legs to control a bucking yearling like she used to. Me, I was lucky I could even stand.

I had braces for my legs and crutches for my arms. I couldn't carry hay or oats to a horse, let alone ride them. Mama had been teaching me everything she knew, but now it was all she could do to take care of her own horses and me.

The trainers and their thoroughbreds went away as did the money from Mama's colts and fillies winning stakes races every racing season. Mama got rehired at the restaurant, so we could keep the few horses she still owned. I was home with my schoolwork and nothing else to do with my time. I was way behind in school, so Mama was trying to homeschool me and catch me up with my grade. She hadn't finished high school, but she insisted I would.

I was bored as anything and very depressed about my life. I was relearning to walk with the pins in my legs and with the crutches. My only escape during the day was struggling through a walk down one of the flat riding paths. Back when I could ride a horse down those paths, I wasn't allowed to go into the woods or near the lake. Those were Mama's rules, and I was supposed to follow them or she'd ground me. But the lake was so serene as I limped toward it, and I needed a break anyway.

That was when I met Blue, the crazy horse reading over my shoulder who doesn't know how to respect a private diary. Of course, he tried to kill me then. I think now might be my turn to return the favor.

*

Rin put his pencil down and turned his head to glare at Blue, who was shamelessly reading over his shoulder. Blue looked totally unrepentant, and he grinned when he caught Rin's glare.

Blue was...blue. It was the best way to describe him. His hair was blue, his eyes were blue, and his lips were faintly blue too. His hair was very long, brushing his knees when he was standing, but the color was an even shade of navy no mere dye could reproduce. At the moment he had his hair pulled into a braid that showed off the pointed tips of his ears and his wide eyes.

You writing anything fun? Blue asked. He didn't speak using sounds; rather, his voice appeared inside Rin's head. Mama couldn't hear Blue, but she was usually busy with the demon horse these days and had long ago given up trying to figure Blue out.

"I'm writing personal things," Rin replied, letting his glare intensify to emphasize his point. He only wrote to get his thoughts in order, but it was still supposed to be private.

Oh, fun. Blue reached out to yank Rin's diary off the table and pulled it close so he could read it better.

"Hey!" Rin snapped. He grabbed his diary back and clutched it to his chest—as if that would stop Blue from reading it later.

Share.

Rin shook his head violently, holding the diary tighter in his hands.

Share, Blue insisted again. He stepped forward, looming over Rin as ominously as he could with a playful smile on his face.

"No way," Rin replied. He shot to his feet, carefully dodging around Blue and running out of his bedroom. He clambered down the stairs into the kitchen and rushed out the back door into the yard.

Blue let him run, damn him. The fact that Rin could run at all was thanks to hours and hours of exhausting physical therapy. It was hard work Rin knew Blue respected above everything else, so he always let Rin run unfettered. Rin was around the house and halfway across the expansive yard when Blue shot by him at a speed Rin wouldn't have been able to match even without a permanent injury. Blue's long legs stretched out over the hard-packed dirt with ease. He got to the end of the yard and doubled back to circle around Rin, prancing and hopping as his eyes danced with excitement.

Do I get to see?

"Nope."

Wanna see. Wanna see.

"Ugh, Blue, no!" Rin groaned.

Pleeeeaaaasssseeee? I asked nicely! Blue looked so pitiful Rin almost relented. His eyes were large and puppylike, and his lower lip was pouting and shaking slightly. Rin's grip on his diary loosened. It wasn't as if he were writing about something Blue didn't already know.

Half of what he was planning to write, Blue had been present for. Still, a diary was a private thing.

Before Rin could decide, a scream echoed out of the barn. Equine and full of aggression and rage, it was followed by a violent bang and Mama's voice shouting. The journal tumbled from his nerveless fingers as he spun on one heel and sprinted toward the barn.

Blue dashed through the wide barn doors well ahead of Rin. Rin hurried into the dim interior seconds later. Blue had one hand held out toward Demon's nose and was snorting and neighing emphatically in response to whatever Demon was saying.

Demon was an enormous horse, standing a full seventeen hands, and was dark black in color. His paperwork said he was a blue roan, but his coat had darkened with age to the extent that the white hairs were hard to see. At the moment, his teeth were bared and his tail was high. He snorted and pawed at the hay-covered ground in his stall, but he at least wasn't rearing or trying to kick Blue.

Mama was standing deeper in the barn. She was scowling and her arms were crossed. She didn't look hurt, and this wasn't the first time Demon had acted up, but she also didn't look particularly happy. Rin let Blue deal with Demon as he hurried over to her.

The far side of Demon's stall had a hoof-sized hole in the wood. Mama was glaring at the hole with a good bit of exasperation. That would have to be patched and sanded. Demon was aptly named, but he had been with them for over two years. Usually that was more than enough time for Mama to at least begin gentling an angry horse.

Demon lifted a rear hoof and lightly struck the wood next to the hole. Blue snarled, the first noise he had made that didn't sound horselike. Demon's tail lowered slightly, from attack position to alert to a threat position. Blue wasn't someone to be trifled with, no matter how much Demon thought he was the herd leader here.

"Well, damn," Mama sighed, her heavy Southern twang filling the barn. "Blue, when you've finished threatening that beast into submission, throw him out in the empty paddock." She looked at the hole in the stall again and shook her head. "Rin, come help me get some wood to patch this mess up." She stomped out of the barn, and Rin followed. Blue had Demon under control for the moment.

Demon was the result of an act of desperation on the part of Mama and his annoyed owner, Wesley of Wesley and Solomon Stables. He was a stakes winner, but he was also an asshole. If he felt like running, no horse in the field could keep up with him. If he didn't feel like running, no jockey could stay on him. Rin had heard Wesley ran out of jockeys who would even try. Demon's injury count outweighed the lure of prize money. Racehorses were high-strung in general—Rin knew that all too well—but Demon was in a dangerous class of his own. Mr. Wesley had decided to retire Demon and pair him up with some gentle mares in the hope that Demon's foals would be tenable.

A full dossier had arrived with Demon, and Rin had read it. The short of it was no other owner had been willing to put their mares to Demon, so Wesley had tried with some of his own, but Demon savaged the mares instead of mating with them. Wesley could have tried tranquilizing Demon and using artificial insemination, but by this point Demon's reputation as a sire was also ruined. If Wesley wanted a willing buyer for one of Demon's foals, or a jockey willing to ride one, he would need to deal with Demon's attitude first. As a last resort, Wesley had turned to Mama. She had gentled two of his horses before and had a good reputation among owners and trainers, so having her name attached to Demon's would solve the negative perceptions issue, and he'd hoped Mama could get some foals from Demon when no one else could.

Plus, Wesley knew about the problems Mama had been having just keeping the roof over their heads. It grated on Rin to admit this, but it would cost Wesley less to take advantage of Mama's desperation than any of the more expensive or time-consuming options. He had sent Demon to Mama and had then probably chosen to forget about the beast except for when he had to write the check to pay for Demon's boarding. Mama couldn't handle the expense of that without Wesley's money, especially considering she already had two horses of her own to take care of, and they definitely weren't cheap.

Demon, the first horse Mama had taken in since the accident, had been methodically destroying the barn for the last two years. There was enough money tied up with the endeavor that Mama could start rebuilding her business. Except, even she couldn't get Demon to behave. Without Blue, she would have lost Demon months ago.

Wesley was angry it had taken so long and even Mama hadn't gotten a foal out of Demon yet, and his irate phone calls were now coming weekly instead of monthly. Still, Wesley didn't want anything to do with Demon any longer, so he didn't want Demon returned. He wanted a foal with Demon's racing abilities with as little of his own effort in the process as possible. Two years was nothing to wait for a foal, although heading into three or four was getting a bit ridiculous given what Mama had been capable of in the past. They had to figure Demon out now so they could get that needed foal and the money that went with it. Rin's summer job only brought in enough to help out; rehabilitating Demon was the only way they would finally be able to dig themselves out of the hole they were in.

There were some two-by-fours in one of the sheds in the yard. To properly fix the stall, they would need to pull out the destroyed bits of wood and properly replace the whole back side of the stall with new wood, but there was no way they could afford that right now. A quick patch would have to do until they got some money coming in again. Or Rin could quit his summer job and get a full-time one, but the last time he suggested that, he'd made

Mama frown—the kind of frown that said she was holding back tears so he wouldn't see how badly she hated that she couldn't provide for her family. He hadn't dared bring it up again, but if things kept going the way they were, he wouldn't have a choice soon.

He collected his dropped diary on the way to grab some nails and a hammer while Mama got the wood. Rin took a few extra seconds alone in the shed as he collected his supplies to push those dark thoughts to the back of his mind. When he walked out into the yard, his own unhappy frown was gone. Demon was galloping around the paddock, neighing angrily at the top of his lungs. Blue was leaning on the fence watching him, but he turned and trotted over to Rin when Rin returned to the yard with his tools.

Not a happy horsie. Blue was frowning over his shoulder at the still-bugling Demon, but then he shrugged and turned away. *I'm going swimming. Wanna come?*

Rin couldn't hide a smile. Even Demon acting up couldn't change the fact that Blue really loved swimming. It was early summer and warm; swimming didn't sound bad at all. "Let me finish patching that hole first," Rin replied.

Blue paced excitedly at Rin's side as Rin headed back into the barn. Mama was already measuring a couple pieces of wood to see what would fit over the hole. Once she gentled Demon, she would be able to afford to do more than only patch up the messes. She would also be able to pay off all those damned red notices she thought she could hide from him. Every cent of the money that would come in from Demon was already allocated, but getting Demon back on track would hopefully bring in more business, and those checks would keep coming.

Mama looked up when Rin walked to her side and added the hammer and a box of nails to the pile on the floor. Her eyes switched to Blue, who was hopping impatiently behind Rin, and she grinned.

"Go swim, you scamps." She laughed. "I can finish this on my own."

Blue squealed a happy horse sound and spun around to run out of the barn.

"Thanks, Mama," Rin said. He paused to double-check she was telling the truth. Her smile widened and she waved him on. Rin hurried out of the barn after Blue, who was waiting in the middle of the yard. As Rin watched, Blue's body shimmered, and a second later, a gigantic blue horse stood in the yard. He wasn't blue like Demon; instead, he was a darker, dun-toned blue. Of course, that was only if Rin described Blue using modern horse identifications. There wasn't any white or black in Blue's coat at all, which made his coloring technically impossible.

But Blue wasn't exactly a normal horse: two small, pointed horns poked up next to his perky ears, which were longer and pointier than on a normal horse. Blue neighed in impatience as Rin headed toward him, and Rin saw the pair of sharp canines in Blue's mouth.

Come on! Swimming time!

Rin laughed and picked up the pace to reach Blue, tossing his diary safely onto the front porch of the house as he went past. He put one hand high on Blue's shoulder, and a shiver of magic ran through his fingers. He pulled on his hand experimentally and couldn't move it away from Blue at all. Blue's magic was designed to keep even the most unwilling victims on his back. Rin pushed on his hand to get leverage and managed to swing one leg up onto Blue's high back. Without the extra-sticky magic holding his hand in place, Rin didn't think he would have had the strength in his legs to get on at all. Blue jumped a little, and Rin's hand came unstuck as his body was jostled into place. The shiver of magic returned, this time in his thighs as he bent forward to take a double handful of Blue's mane.

"Let's go!"

Blue's laugh sounded happy in Rin's mind as he reared in the air with a loud whinny. His front feet hit the ground, and they were off. Some of the old riding trails on their property were overgrown from disuse, but the path to the lake was clear.

Rin didn't need powerful leg muscles to stay on Blue. He didn't have to move with Blue's steps to shift his weight appropriately. In fact, it was nothing like riding a real horse, which was good because Rin's bad legs wouldn't let him. Blue's magic had returned his ability to ride, which was amazing, but he didn't quite dare try it with other horses. Truthfully, Blue was the one and only horse Rin wanted to ride these days. His legs shook in remembered pain merely at the idea of putting them through the rigors of riding a real horse.

They arrived at the lake swiftly. Blue ran right into the water without stopping. Rin floated free from Blue's back as the magic released and Blue dove deep. Rin swam to shore to take off his soaked boots. The sand quickly seeped into places it shouldn't as he fought with wet shoelaces and got his shirt off.

Blue beached himself next to Rin, soaking him again with a wave of water. *You coming?* Blue asked, sounding reproachful that Rin had gotten out of the water. His front hooves had gained four short, webbed claws. His rear legs had vanished entirely, replaced by what Rin could best describe as a lightly furred mermaid's tail. Blue was scary, but beautiful in his most natural form. Luckily, he'd decided not to eat Rin.

Rin shucked his pants, keeping his boxers on, and rushed into the water. Blue whinnied and rushed after him, pouncing with a laugh when Rin spluttered. Rin pounced back, shoving Blue underwater. Blue dove, whapping Rin with his tail as he went.

Blue's laughter followed Rin as he swam farther out in the lake, relaxing under the warm sun in the cool water while the kelpie frolicked below him.

*

It was only a short half mile to the lake. I had walked that far in slow progress on the special treadmill at physical therapy, and I didn't see any reason why I couldn't do that on my own. Not that I was actually planning to go to the lake specifically. It was just a good landmark to turn around at. Mama would yell endlessly if I went near the lake, especially since there was no way I could swim with my destroyed legs and the braces on them.

It was harder to walk on the uneven ground of the pockmarked path than on a flat treadmill. I managed to avoid the worst of the hoof-scarred holes in the ground from all the horses I had ridden down the same path only a few months before the accident. If I had tripped and fallen, I'm not certain I could have gotten back up without help.

I had fixed my gaze on the lake as I walked. My legs felt like wet noodles before I was even halfway there, which to be honest was a slight improvement over blinding pain. I was still walking. That was all that mattered to me in that moment.

I still don't know how I made it to the lake. Looking back on that walk and the terrible condition my body was in, I know it shouldn't have been possible. But at the same time, my life was in shambles around me. I couldn't return to school to hang out with my friends; they were all a grade ahead of me and starting to think about preparing for college or getting jobs while I was stuck in bed most of the day. I couldn't ride horses any longer, which I had loved. I couldn't even help Mama take care of the horses! She would come home every night after a long day waitressing and still have to feed and exercise the horses while I sat around and watched.

A strange sort of desperation filled me during that walk to the lake. I would get to the lake and prove my body wasn't useless, that I was getting better and stronger, and soon enough I could return to how my life should have been before the accident. I could do at least that much.

When I reached the small beach, I collapsed with no strength left in my legs. Moments later, I passed out.

The path I had been following continued to the left, turning sharply away from the lake and the forest that bordered the far bank. The lake itself had always been calm and serene, almost too inviting, but I had been on an excitable horse before and had never had the chance to sit on the beach and relax. Besides, Mama always said I should stay away from the lake.

When I woke, there was a horse staring at me. Wanna swim? it asked me as if there wasn't even a tiny chance I would disagree.

I saw the snack lying on the beach. I wanted to eat him.

Blue! Stay out of my diary!

But you were delicious-looking! Except, when I left the water, you were covered in metal. Too scrawny too. I thought I could at least eat some bone marrow.

Mama will have dinner ready soon, Blue. Stop drooling on the pages! Why are we even writing to each other like this?

*

"Damn it, Blue," Rin whined. He shut his diary with a thump to cover the fact that he was feeling silly for having a written conversation with Blue when they were sitting next to each other on Rin's bed.

Still not much meat, Blue grumbled. He pinched Rin's arm contemplatively, studying the flesh between his fingers with a frown. *Not good eating, but you're definitely still delicious.*

"Should I be worried you're going to take a bite out of me in my sleep?" Rin asked, only half joking. When Blue's stomach growled, he couldn't help worrying a bit.

Blue grinned, his smile wide and pointy. His eyes showed only mirth, but as always, it wasn't a concrete answer.

One day eat, one day not eat. He shrugged. *Depends on what Mama's got for dinner.* And that wasn't reassuring at all. Blue's widening smile told Rin that Blue was well aware of his ambiguity and loving it. At the very least, Rin was pretty certain Blue would only eat him in an absolute emergency.

"Boys, come set the table please." Mama's voice sounded up the stairs.

Rin tucked his diary away on a bookshelf and followed Blue out of his room and down the stairs. Mama was standing in front of the stove tending two pans, one full of oil and sizzling french fries, the other filled with hamburger patties frying away. The outdoor grill was out of propane again, and until they got Mama's paycheck from the restaurant, they couldn't afford to fill it. Burgers on the stove weren't bad though.

She's cooking the meat again, Blue grumbled. He made a whining sound in his throat as he padded over to stare over Mama's shoulder at the burgers in the pan.

"Look in the fridge, Blue," Mama said without looking up. She was smiling slightly as she stirred the fries. Rin reached around her to grab three plates from the cabinet over the stove while Blue hurried over to the fridge, yanked it open, stuck his head inside, and then squealed a moment later as he pulled out a plate covered in plastic wrap. Blue spun around the kitchen with the plate in his hands, still squealing, and then plunked the plate down at his spot at the table and ripped the covering off.

Two large hamburger patties sat on his plate, the meat still raw, and mixed with something green that had been shredded into small pieces. Since the food was for Blue, it was safe to assume Mama had added cucumber.

"Wait for the rest of us," Mama admonished just seconds before Blue's fingers were about to close around one of the patties. Blue whined again, but he sank into his chair where he could stare hungrily at his plate. Rin put two plates in front of the other two chairs and put the third away. He got out cups and silverware, which he added to the table without Blue's help.

Once dinner was ready and they were all sitting at the table, Mama turned to Blue. "Thank you for waiting," she said.

Blue looked up from staring at his plate to look at her. He licked his lips and whined in question.

Hungry. Wanna eat.

"Let's eat," Mama finished, her smile growing at Blue. Blue immediately grabbed one of the patties in his hands and ripped a large chunk off with his sharp teeth. Rin filled his plate with a cooked burger on a bun, some fries, ketchup, and a small handful of sliced cucumbers from a bowl Mama had added to the table when Blue wasn't looking. Mama took her own food, including the cucumbers, and then plunked the mostly full bowl next to Blue's plate.

Blue looked up, let out another happy squeal, and promptly added a layer of sliced cucumbers to the top of his red, dripping, raw hamburger. Rin had long ago learned not to watch Blue eat.

"The farrier is coming tomorrow morning," Mama said once they had slowed down enough to speak without food in their mouths. "I'm not sedating Demon, so hopefully that beast doesn't need his hooves checked, but I'll need Mary and Tildie brought from the far paddock first thing in the morning."

Yet another expense they couldn't afford not to take if they wanted their horses to be healthy. Instead of mentioning that, Rin asked, "Can we leave the mares so close to Demon?"

"I'm going to get him in the barn and get that all locked up, so he won't be able to see or smell them until after the farrier is gone," Mama said.

Blue looked up from where he was piling more cucumbers onto his second burger. *I'll help*, he offered.

"Blue says he'll help," Rin repeated, so Mama could hear.

*

The snack was breathing, so at least the meat wasn't spoiled yet. I could see that through the water. One rip of my claws and the snack would be mine. It wasn't moving much either. An injured snack was easier to catch! It wouldn't be satisfying though. The best snacks took a ride into the water with me first. Maybe I should wait for this snack to wake up?

But he looked so delicious! I wanted to eat now.

I crawled up the sand to the snack's side and gave it a good sniff. It smelled tired and hurt, like perfect pickings, and oh so delicious. I wanted to eat it right away.

Then the eyes opened. They were blue, my favorite color, and they focused right on me. I called on my glamour. I am a very pretty horsie, yes I am. You want to get on my back, yes you do. So I can drown you and eat your waterlogged flesh. That sounds fun, right?

I couldn't help asking, Wanna swim, as if the snack could actually hear me. Snacks couldn't hear my voice. That's why they're snacks!

But this snack answered.

"I can't swim right now. Why is there a loose horse around here anyway?" He sounded halfway to screaming from pain, but also too tired to let it out. I could eat him now, and he'd never know he had woken up. But he could hear me.

Why no swimming? I asked. Getting him onto my back and into the water would still be best.

He twitched one of his legs, and I looked down to see.

Back then, all I could see were the ugly silver metal rods and hinges locked around his knees and lower legs. The skin was red and abraded-looking with scarred holes where stitches had been removed and puckered marks where bone had recently poked through.

The metal would burn me if I tried to get it off on my own. Normally, a touch of glamor would get a snack to take off all the burning parts, but this snack was different. He wasn't listening to my magic and instead was listening to my actual voice. I sat at his side for a few seconds, totally indecisive. I could still kill him and eat him even though I would have to avoid his legs. He would be a very good snack. But he was so different from anyone else who had wandered near my lake. For some weird reason, I didn't want to eat him.

He passed out again while I was thinking. His breathing was hitched with pain, and there were lines between his brows. He shouldn't be lying on a beach, so far from his own home.

I shifted into a more human form and gathered him in my arms. He was too light for someone his size, and his broken legs hung limply to the side, but it wasn't difficult to follow the path leading to the farmhouse.

*

Rin stirred awake in bed and wondered why there was light reflecting on the wall in front of him. He rolled over and saw his small desk lamp was on. It was barely bright enough to irritate him. He hadn't left it on when he'd gone to bed, and since the other person who slept in his bed was missing, it was easy enough to guess what was going on.

When he sat up, he found Blue sitting in the desk chair with Rin's diary open in front of him.

"Blue," Rin groaned. Somehow the damned kelpie had gotten hooked on Rin's diary to the extent that he was skipping sleep to play with it. It honestly wasn't worth fighting over anymore. "Come to bed. We have a lot to do in the morning."

Blue put down his pencil and closed the journal before shutting out the light and returning to bed. He climbed under the covers and draped his body over Rin's. He was warm and heavy, and as comfortable as curling up with a toasty quilt. Rin wrapped his arms around Blue and drifted back to sleep to the sound of Blue's happy rumbling purr in his ear.

The alarm clock sounded a few hours later. Rin groaned and opened his eyes. The sun was just beginning to shine through his bedroom window as dawn took over from night. It was early, but there were mares to feed and Demon to wrangle.

Blue grumbled, still mostly asleep. His face was buried in Rin's shoulder, his sharp teeth gently gnawing on Rin's skin. Blue did that a lot, like a baby chewing on his pacifier when he was getting hungry. He somehow managed to never break the skin, so Rin didn't complain. It was just Blue.

Rin had originally thought that, from his coloring and his love of water, Blue would feel cold and clammy, but the exact opposite was true. Blue was a warm and welcome weight lying on top of Rin, even when he bit a little too hard.

Blue growled lightly under his breath when Rin shifted. His tongue licked a long stripe over Rin's shoulder, and he wiggled his hips. His weight pushing Rin into the bed sent a shiver down Rin's spine and a heat that settled even lower.

Blue's tongue dragged up the side of Rin's neck, which made Rin shiver and twitch his hips so his growing bulge could press against Blue. Blue growled again at Rin's movement, and his arms tightened around Rin's body.

Silly snack, Blue's sleep-roughened voice sounded inside Rin's head. *Shall we try another kind of eating?*

Blue sat up, and there was nothing innocent about the look in his eyes as he took in Rin lying below him. Blue shifted slightly over Rin, and suddenly their hips were aligned. Blue's hardness pressed deliciously against Rin's, sending a shiver of want up Rin's spine. Blue leaned down slowly until his face was inches above Rin's. He grinned, flashing his pointed teeth, before licking across Rin's lips with another swipe of his tongue.

Yum.

Rin's lips were slimy and wet from spit and it was gross, but his body responded all the same. He wanted a proper kiss though. Rin reached out to cup Blue's head in both hands, drawing him gently downward again. This time there was no tongue or teeth, just lips pressed against lips and the heavy emotion swirling between them.

"Hey, you miscreants!" Mama yelled through the door, banging on it forcefully, and making them both jump in surprise. "Time for breakfast. Get up or don't get fed."

Blue whined and huffed out a snort through his nose. *I'm going to eat her.*

"You will not," Rin grumbled back. Mama had effectively banished all the ardor in the room. Blue rolled off Rin and flipped off the covers. He was wearing only a pair of thin navy pajama pants. They didn't leave much to the imagination and highlighted the blue hair of his happy trail for Rin to drool over. Blue wandered off in the direction of the bathroom, which gave Rin a few moments to catch his breath.

Blue was a force to be reckoned with. That was certain. It was only a matter of time before kissing and bodies pressing together became more. Rin was looking forward to it, of course, but he was also afraid. What would it mean for their relationship? It had taken long enough to get Blue to come into the house and to trust him. Being intimate could ruin all of that—could destroy their friendship if it went bad—and as much as Rin loved Blue, he didn't know if he was ready to take that chance.

Rin climbed out of bed and headed to his dresser to pull out a fresh pair of jeans and a shirt. When Blue wandered back in a few minutes later, naked with his hair dripping water all over the floor, Rin averted his eyes and hurried to the bathroom for his own shower. Blue's body was perfectly proportioned, and he had no shame. He also didn't understand why Rin didn't share that shamelessness. It was something Rin had gotten used to about Blue, but Blue naked with water droplets dripping down his leanly muscled body was still an image that imprinted itself on Rin's brain.

Blue's voice humming happily in Rin's head didn't help Rin's erection fade in the least either as he walked down the hall with his clothes held awkwardly in front of his crotch. He locked the bathroom door behind him to keep Blue and Mama from wandering inside and left his clothes by the door. It didn't take him long once he had himself in hand. The water was warm in the shower from Blue's recent use, and Rin let the spray pound on his back as his fist pumped. He stifled his gasps in his arm, but he still heard Blue's humming change to an interested whinny. The sound sent Rin over the edge. He shot hard, hitting the floor of the tub and letting the water wash it all away.

After panting for a few long minutes to catch his breath, Rin grabbed the soap and got clean. Blue's humming faded once Rin was done. He dried off and got dressed before leaving the bathroom to dump his pajamas in the laundry bag in his room.

Blue was sitting on the bed, looking petulant. *You never let me join you*, he grumbled with a pout.

"We'll get there, Blue," Rin replied truthfully. One morning Mama wouldn't interrupt.

Blue's frown almost immediately turned into a knowing grin. There were the times when Blue seemed to be much older than Rin despite the fact he looked like he was in his early twenties. Right now, with that grin on his face, Blue looked like he had much more experience at this than Rin did. Rin didn't know how long kelpies lived, but it was very possible Rin wasn't Blue's first romantic relationship.

Rin bent and pressed his lips against Blue's. He knew what he was promising and sealing with a kiss, and he was okay with that.

"It's getting cold!" Mama yelled up the stairs.

Rin grimaced and pulled away. "I guess we should go eat?"

Fluffy squawker eggs! Blue agreed happily. He had only seen a live chicken once, but he had called them that ever since. Rin grinned and led the way to the kitchen.

*

Ever since the day I woke up on my couch after dreaming about a beautiful blue horse who wanted to eat me, I felt like someone was watching me. Most of the time it wasn't a problem. Mama was usually around whenever I went outside. She was with the horses, of course, but she always kept an eye on me as I made slow progress through the yard. Every day showed slight improvement in my walking ability, but winter was coming, and the doctors had already warned me repeatedly that slipping on ice could set back my recovery drastically. I wanted to be as sure on my feet as possible before the weather turned so I could avoid that problem.

During the day, Mama was at work at the restaurant and I was left to my own ends like usual. My memories of walking to the lake were shaky. I knew I had gotten there, but I had no idea how I had gotten home. I did know just how badly my legs had ached and trembled for days afterward, which kept me from trying that adventure again. I stayed in the yard when Mama wasn't home, practicing putting my feet down properly so I would build muscle and muscle memory.

The eyes watching me were constant whenever I stepped outside. In a strange way, it was comforting to know someone was watching over me, but it still made the hair on the back of my neck lift in fear. Sometimes the stare felt dangerously hungry, and other times innocently curious.

I thought about telling Mama about it, but I would also have to explain walking to the lake. I was still young enough to be afraid of her punishment—a few months past turning sixteen—and didn't want to admit I'd broken her rules. Besides, what could she do about a water horse that was stalking me?

I spent a lot more time than I ordinarily would have indoors working on my schoolwork that fall, but even that didn't keep the eyes away. The days began to cool and the leaves in the forest in the distance turned colors and every day there was someone unseen looking in the windows at me, blinking curiously at everything I was doing.

Mama was happy I was beginning to catch up to my grade level, although I still finished high school at the kitchen table without ever returning to a classroom. I didn't care so much about my schoolwork at that point in my life, too depressed about being hurt to care about much at all. I wanted to be out there helping Mama with the horses, not stuck inside. However, for the first time since the accident, I found myself interested in something. The mystery of a horse who could talk and wanted to watch me struggle over math problems day after day was strange enough that it pulled me out of my permanent funk. At least, I hoped it was that horse. I'm sure Mama was happy to see me finally smile again, although at the time she didn't know why.

One cool fall day, I zipped up my coat and took my homework outside to the porch. Whoever was watching me had plenty of opportunity to do something awful to me. I was a sitting duck since I couldn't run and no one was home during the day to hear me scream, yet I was only observed. I honestly felt safe enough in the open, even as those eyes continued to watch my every move.

I was wearing my winter coat and heavy pants to keep the metal braces on my legs from freezing by the time I met Blue. The yard had iced over during a light snowfall after breakfast. Mama had gotten the chains on her car tires so she could head to work, and I decided to take my walk early before the weather changed for the worse. Not my brightest idea.

Two feet into the yard, and I went flying. Arms pinwheeling, me yelping and sliding across the ice. I was in for a hard and painful fall, and with Mama gone I would've had to figure out a way to get myself back into the house before I froze and died. I doubt all of that ran through my mind at the time, but it was true, nonetheless. Except instead of me hitting the ground, Blue caught me. His arms wrapped around me, and he pulled me to his warm chest to steady me. I looked at his startled face, as if he was as surprised by his actions as I was, and I knew I was safe.

Was I pretty?

"Damn it, Blue," Rin groaned, looking at Blue's handwriting in the margin next to his last journal entry. He had just wanted to quickly read through what he had written so he didn't skip anything. Apparently Blue had already helped himself to Rin's private journal. Again.

Rin looked at the three short words Blue had written, sighed, and scrawled *Yes* underneath. Blue might be a damned conceited kelpie, but he was pretty. There was no denying that. His big blue eyes, the horns sticking out of his blue hair, and the long and pointed ears had all pegged him as something other than human that first day, but despite that, Rin remembered that moment with as much lust as when Blue had been walking around naked earlier that morning. It was love at first sight, at least once Rin had stopped being shocked by a mystical creature holding him safely and gently guiding him onto the dry porch where he could collect his footing again. That Blue had disappeared for a week afterward before creeping back as if he couldn't help himself hadn't mattered to Rin in the least.

Blue was bugling outside, a noise that sounded more like elk than horse—although Rin would never, ever tell Blue that—so Rin moved to the window to look out. Mary and Tildie were still in the paddock. Mama had gone to work before moving them back to the far pasture to give them some time to relax after having their hooves filed down. Maryquitecontrary and Till the Cows Come Home had been their prospective racing names before the accident. They had never gotten the chance to race and had never stepped foot onto a track to prove their mettle, but they were good breeding stock all the same. Mama had high hopes for them both. Blue was talking to them over the fence. Mary was doing her best to ignore him, hence his bugling, but Tildie seemed interested.

Rin had to agree with Tildie. He abandoned his diary at the desk and hurried downstairs.

*

I had never touched a human before. Okay, I had eaten plenty of them. Their bones are nice and crunchy, and the muscles aren't as stringy as some of the other critters I had eaten. They are much better than fish. Fish is slimy.

All right, I'll admit I touched one human. I had carried him home when he collapsed on my beach. But this human, this snack, was different. I had been spying and watching since then. He couldn't walk; he was the injured member of the herd and good pickings, yet he didn't hide or cower. Instead he sat outside and read from lots of different books while the cold came.

I wasn't going to eat him. I don't know when I decided that, but my tummy didn't rumble whenever I was around him.

Snow fell, and ice. And he went sliding across the ground. I don't remember moving, but suddenly he was in my arms.

Chapter Two

My daddy wasn't a cowboy. At least, I don't think he was. Hell, my daddy probably wasn't even human. He had to be someone like Blue, human in appearance when he wanted to be, but unable to hide his other nature. The day I brought Blue home, a few short weeks after he caught me, Mama had lifted one eyebrow, swore while shaking her head in exasperation, and told me I had too much of my father in me.

That was the first time I realized maybe one of the reasons Mama had hopped on that train north when she was pregnant with me was because she wasn't certain whether I would come out with horns like Blue. Her parents would have drowned me in the river as a devil's child had that happened. Mama has never told me who my father is or what he looks like, but she had apparently spent enough time with him to understand the ways Blue would be different from a regular human. I used to think she hadn't spent much time with my father, but now that I think about how she treated Blue... It tells me they were definitely together longer than I'd suspected.

I remember wondering at the time whether I might be able to change shape or something special. There were times when, instead of doing my homework, I would sit on the porch trying to find that other shape somewhere inside myself. I wanted to have magic of some sort, even if it wasn't as cool as what Blue could do, but despite all of my attempts and even some begging for Blue to explain how he did it—which he hadn't really been able to put into words I could understand—I still couldn't change my shape. I will admit to some disappointment over that fact, but at the same time, having Blue around had brought more than enough magic into my life.

Mama put sheets on the bed in the guest bedroom and another plate at the dinner table without comment, and then cooked us all dinner. She didn't even grumble when Blue complained about his meat being ruined, just pulled out another portion to serve him raw. She did throw a fit when she realized that Blue wasn't sleeping in the guest bedroom.

Mama realized that before even me. Blue slept in my desk chair for the first two weeks instead of the guest bedroom, as Mama pointed out loudly. As he slowly grew more comfortable with the fact that I fascinated him, he moved to the bed.

You were just as fascinated!

Rin dropped his pen onto his desk with a roll of his eyes. Could he write anything without Blue adding his own comments? Obviously not, but Rin should have expected that. Besides, Blue was telling the truth. He had wondered endlessly about whoever was watching him for weeks and weeks while he struggled through his homework, and that fascination didn't stop because Blue had finally introduced himself and Mama had let him stay while his lake was frozen over.

It had taken a while for Mama to come to terms with the fact that Blue was male and he and Rin were sharing a bed. With her usual level of perceptiveness, she realized before Rin did that he and Blue had feelings for each other. Rin knew her reticence about gay people was a terrible holdover from her time in the South, and Mama tried to be understanding about it, but it was a tough time for all of them, what with Blue discovering there were humans he didn't want to eat, Rin discovering his libido hadn't died with the accident like he'd thought it had, and Mama throwing off more of her past so she could embrace the present with an open mind.

Three years had passed since. Blue hadn't returned to his lake with the thaw, and Mama hadn't asked him to. These days, Blue was practically her second son. Hell, Mama probably assumed Rin and Blue had had sex multiple times. She didn't understand that swimming was more important to Blue than sex, which had kept them from doing it at the lake, and that nighttime up until now had been about sleeping. It was in the morning that the good stuff happened, when Rin's defenses were lowered and Blue was extra frisky, yet Mama always managed to interrupt before they got anywhere. She was crafty like that.

Rin stood up from his desk before his thoughts could continue in that direction. He shut the journal on Blue's last words without answering them and stowed the journal on the bookshelf where Blue could find it later.

The sun was still high in the sky even as the smell of Mama cooking dinner wafted up the stairs. Midsummer was approaching far too fast. The days were long and hot, Blue's lake cool and crisp, and the cloud of Rin's seasonal job was hanging over everyone. He didn't want to have to leave the house to go to the job—Blue certainly didn't want Rin to leave—but they needed the money he would bring in.

Mama probably needed help setting the table, so Rin pushed away those unhappy thoughts and headed downstairs. Blue wasn't in the kitchen looking over Mama's shoulders while she sliced cucumbers, which meant he was still outside. Rin snuck past Mama so she wouldn't hand him a spatula and tell him to get to work and went out the back door.

If the front of the house belonged to the horses, with the three large barns, two paddocks, and all the sheds circled around the yard, the back of the house belonged to Blue. Mama had originally decided not to build anything there because she wanted an open space for Rin to play as he grew up. She kept the horses out of the backyard, which meant Rin could play to his heart's content without worrying about stepping in something gross or getting trampled. After the accident, they'd barely used any of the space in the front for the horses, and Rin had been too hurt to use the yard.

Then Blue had arrived.

One day in the middle of spring, not even a year after Blue had moved in, Mama had come home with a packet of seeds and instructions for Blue. Rin and Blue had turned the earth and planted the seeds, and Blue had been amazed to watch cucumbers grow. The garden had expanded a bit since. Mama had her carrots and beans growing on one side of the yard, but the vast majority of the backyard had been turned into small hills with green cucumber shoots growing up tomato trellises. It was a big deal in the house every year when the first flowers appeared.

When Rin found him, Blue was crooning softly to a thumb-sized cucumber slowly growing. One of Blue's ears flicked in Rin's direction, so Blue knew Rin was there, but he finished his song before turning to grin at Rin.

So, so many cucumbers! he exclaimed happily. *I want to eat them!*

"Give them one more week, Blue," Rin replied with a smile. Blue was at his cutest when he was happy. "Have you finished singing to them?"

Not singing, Blue grumped. *I'm telling them to grow big and delicious so I can eat them. And I have one more hill.*

Rin laughed. "Finish quickly. I think Mama's going to be calling us to dinner soon."

Blue nodded and returned to his cucumbers. Rin watched for a few moments as Blue caressed each growing vegetable and touched each blooming flower. It was beautiful, if slightly creepy. It was like Blue was singing to a baby just moments before tossing it into a pot of boiling water. Definitely creepy, which didn't quite explain why Rin was getting slightly horny watching Blue gently caress cucumbers.

The beans probably needed to be picked, Rin told himself as he forced himself to turn away and walk to the other side of the garden. He bent down to check the pole beans Mama had growing on another trellis.

"What have you done?" a voice snarled. Rin jumped in surprise, his foot landing mere inches away from crushing one of the plants under his feet, and looked up. A man was standing in the middle of the backyard, only a few feet from the garden. He hadn't been there a second ago. "How dare you ensnare one of our innocents for your cruel purposes!"

"What?" Rin asked, still gaping in surprise. The speed with which he had appeared coupled with his appearance told Rin the man couldn't be human. He was very tall, even taller than Blue, who topped out at six foot two. His skin was dusky black. Not the dark-brown color of natural human skin, but an eerie, true black. His ears were also pointed, Rin noticed, but it was a much subtler point than Blue's ears.

"Release him at once!" the man growled. He stalked forward, his entire body vibrating with threat. Rin gulped, he couldn't help it, and tried not to take a step back and crush a plant. "Fine. If you won't release him, I'll curse you. I call upon Danu and beseech her: place a geas on—" A hand appeared over the man's mouth before he could finish his sentence.

The air around Rin felt heavy, like a bad storm was just on the horizon, but it dissipated quickly as a breeze blew through the yard. Blue snarled from behind the stranger. His hand over the stranger's mouth had long claws at the end of his normally blunt fingers, and those claws were digging in. Blood dripped down the stranger's neck.

Don't touch my snack, Blue hissed. *He's mine!*

He's enspelled you. I'm here to free you and help you return home!

Rin heard both voices inside his head.

Do I look enspelled to you, idiot drow? He's my snack, and I'm going to eat him, not the other way around.

They were quiet for a few moments, glaring at each other. Rin stepped out from the garden and approached Blue.

"What's going on?" he asked, looking warily at the man Blue had called a drow.

Blue whined and stepped away from the stranger, putting his body directly between Rin and the drow. *He's being mean,* Blue hissed. He growled at the drow again.

"Now look here, both of you," the man said, holding out one hand. Blue tensed.

"Not another move," Mama snarled from behind them. She pumped her shotgun pointedly. Rin didn't turn to look, but he knew Mama must be aiming the gun at the stranger, and she meant business. "Don't you do anything to hurt my kids."

The man slowly dropped his hand. "You're Lizzy Roark?" he asked, sounding surprised.

"And if I am?" Mama snapped in reply.

The drow smiled. "I'm Jim O'Malley from Overhill Stables."

"I know who you are," Mama said. "I also know what you are, dark elf. Get the hell away from my kids!"

Jim's grin faded into a contemplative look. "First off, I'm only half unseelie sidhe, and my seelie father did my rearing. Second, I'm that idiot's guardian." He pointed with his chin at Blue, which was smart since moving his hands would probably get him shot. "Apparently, Blue forgot he sent me a rather cryptic letter asking if I had any gold stashed around my house. When I stopped by his lake and found him missing, I assumed the worst and went hunting for his captors."

Blue had tilted his head curiously as Jim explained, and he sighed when Jim finished. *I forgot*, he admitted. *But you shouldn't have tried to hurt my snack! Rin is mine!*

"Blue," Rin groaned. "Mama, Blue knows him."

Mama snorted. "Of course he does. And now dinner's probably burning because of your damned mix-up." The gun clicked as she popped the safety.

"We can't have that," Jim said smoothly. "How about we all go inside, rescue dinner, and have a little talk about this?"

You won't try to hurt Rin again? Blue asked suspiciously.

I won't, Jim replied in Rin's head, but the cold, wary look in his eyes told Rin he likely meant *Not tonight, at least*.

Blue let out a soft whinny as he spun on one heel. He grabbed Rin's hand in his and pulled Rin along behind him, past Mama and into the house. He let Rin go in the kitchen so Rin could hurry and rescue a pot full of smoking oil before it caught fire. The chicken tenders Mama had been about to deep-fry were still uncooked on a plate beside the oil. Dinner itself wasn't ruined, but with Jim joining them at the table, Rin didn't think their meal was going to be particularly palatable anyway.

Jim walked into the kitchen from the back door and calmly took a seat at the kitchen table. Rin heard Mama in the back closet, locking the shotgun away again. She joined them a few moments later and snorted in disgust when she saw the burnt oil. She left the pan pushed aside on a cool burner, got out a new pan, filled it with fresh oil, and waited for it to heat up.

"So," she said when no one else spoke up. "Rin and Blue, set the table for four." Rin hurried to obey, knowing the clipped tone to her Southern vowels spelled trouble if he didn't. He got four plates out of the cabinet, then put one back when Blue pulled a plastic-wrapped plate full of raw chicken out of the fridge. Blue put his plate on the table in front of his chair and returned to the fridge for the bowl of sliced cucumbers while Rin set the rest of the place settings.

The pop and hiss of the oil as Mama dropped the chicken into it was the only sound in the room. They didn't have french fries to go with the chicken fingers, so Rin found an open bag of potato chips in the pantry. He also got out the tossed salad, the dressing, and a pitcher of water from the fridge that Blue had ignored. With the table set, Rin sat next to Blue to wait for Mama to bring the chicken over.

It didn't take too long for Mama to join them with the rest of the food. Rin took some chicken with homemade honey-mustard sauce, some salad, and some chips as the dishes were passed around. Blue ripped the plastic wrap off his food with his usual exuberance. He picked up one of his pieces of chicken with his hands and bit off an end.

Mama's chicken fingers were dipped in egg, then breaded in cornflake crumbs and spices before they were fried. Blue's were uncooked, but he crunched as much as Rin did as they both chewed. The silence grew even heavier as everyone ate instead of speaking.

Mama put her fork down first. She never could abide by stupidity. "I'll tell you right now, Jim O'Malley, Blue here has been a member of my household since he showed up three years ago clutching at Rin's hand and announcing he was living here now because his lake was frozen over."

"Three years?" Jim gasped, turning to glare at Blue. "I've visited you well over a dozen times in the last three years, and you didn't think to mention that you'd moved into the farmhouse with the human and her kid?"

Rin is mine, and I'm not sharing him! Blue insisted. His face was earnest and intent, and he reached one chicken-sticky hand across the table to grip Rin's previously clean hand.

"No need to translate that one," Mama sighed with a shake of her head.

They finished eating in silence while Jim and Blue glared at each other. Rin switched his fork to his other hand so Blue could continue holding their sticky fingers together. Knowing Blue had been keeping the fact that he had someone who was supposed to watch over him secret wasn't much of a surprise. The way Blue's mind sometimes worked didn't always make sense to Rin, but that was what made Blue unique, and Rin loved that about him. What did have Rin reeling a bit was the way Mama had tossed her knowledge about Jim out so nonchalantly. Jim was a dark elf, she had said, and she hadn't blinked when Jim had corrected her terminology. Rin had no idea what the difference between an unseelie and a seelie sidhe was, but Mama did. Of course, Mama had taken Blue in with barely a blink too. She made him meals with raw meat without fear he would catch salmonella and had known before Rin that giving Blue cucumbers would make him insanely happy.

Mama knew things about people and creatures that Rin apparently didn't, despite the fact he had long assumed he was partly one of those creatures too. She was taking Jim's presence better than when she had realized Rin and Blue were sharing a bed. It was very disconcerting.

They finished dinner without more conversation. Rin and Blue cleared the table, leaving the dishes next to the sink for Mama to wash. Jim offered to help, but Mama waved him to his seat.

"The beans do need to be picked," Mama said to Rin with a pointed look. She apparently hadn't missed him sneaking past her earlier to join Blue in the garden instead of offering to help with dinner, and she wasn't impressed. "We'll eat them tomorrow if you finish picking tonight."

It was summer. The sun was still high in the sky and wouldn't set for another three hours. Normally Rin and Blue would run off to play or swim until it got dark, but with Jim still sitting at the kitchen table, Rin knew Blue wouldn't want to wander far. Picking the beans was also a good way to get Rin and Blue out of the kitchen for a few minutes so Mama and Jim could talk, so Rin didn't argue. He washed his sticky hands—and made Blue wash too— grabbed a bowl from one of the cabinets, and led the way outside. He left the back door open behind him and stayed nearby where he could overhear their conversation.

"Your horses ride good races," he could barely hear Mama saying to Jim.

"Yours used to. I heard about what happened. It was such a shame you didn't win the Saratoga Trainer's Title that year."

"I came in second while I was in the hospital, and the doctors weren't certain Rin would keep his legs. I had more important things to worry about than coming in first," Mama finished scathingly.

"And yet," Jim said calmly, "it's been years since the accident. I'm surprised you haven't gotten back into racing."

Mama laughed, and Rin cringed. "With what money?" she asked Jim coldly. "Everything I had went to medical bills. I sold almost all my horses just so I could keep my house while Rin suffered through physical therapy. Thanks to my own injury, I can't sit a yearling. You think I can return to the business like this?"

"I think you only need a little help, which is why I'm guessing Blue asked me for gold." Jim sounded very satisfied. Rin glanced over to Blue. Rin hadn't missed the increasing number of unpaid bills or the worried wrinkle deepening between Mama's eyebrows, but he hadn't thought Blue would notice them too. Blue was lost amid his cucumbers again, so Rin didn't ask. "Don't think I missed the stallion in your barn or the two mares in your paddock. You want to try your hand at the Saratoga meet again."

"Did you bother getting a good look at the horse in my barn?" Mama interrupted. "That's Swearing A Blue Streak, also known as Demon Blue. I've got another year to gentle him for breeding, or he'll be sent to a dog-food factory. I don't want any foals out of that monster, but his owner does."

"And when you collect your breeder's fee, you'll have the funds to start rebuilding your breeding stock and to hire people to do your riding for you." Jim's voice was full of understanding. "I get it. But I have a different idea. I owe you for taking care of Blue for three years. I'm sure he's caused you endless problems."

Blue snorted quietly in protest, but he didn't look up from his plants. So, he was listening.

"He's pulled his own weight around the house. I've made sure of that," Mama replied sharply as if Jim were criticizing her parenting.

"But it still can't have been easy with another mouth to feed and body to clothe. Overhill Stables has been around for ninety-five years now, and there's only so many times I can claim to be my own son taking on the reins from my father before someone notices the twin-like resemblance between father and son. I need thirty years with my face and name out of the news, but I don't want to stop racing my horses."

"So, you want me to take your horses and pretend they're my own?" Mama scoffed. "I'm capable of doing this on my own, thank you very much."

"I'm not giving you my trained racehorses," Jim disagreed. "Just a few mares and stallions—as well as the necessary funds to care for them—that will allow you to restart your breeding program. In two years, you'll have plenty of colts and fillies to train and race as well as have enough incoming funds for them. You'll be back on your feet again, and any debt Blue has incurred will be cleared. In thirty years, I would like you to return the favor by giving me a few horses to rebuild Overhill with."

"It's a very generous offer," Mama said hesitantly. "I would bring in my own stock from outside your stable, you understand."

"To strengthen the bloodlines," Jim replied with perfect understanding. "There's a lot of details to work out. For now, how about I ship in one of my mares? She'll be going into heat soon. If you put her into a paddock with Demon, she'll beat him into learning some manners, and that bastard Wesley can suck it."

Mama laughed. She actually laughed. Rin couldn't help scowling at that. There had been so many years where she could barely crack a smile as Rin struggled and the bills piled up, and Jim could make her laugh so easily. It was infuriating. Not only that, but he was offering an easy solution to the problems that had haunted Rin and Mama for years. Rin couldn't help wondering what Jim was really after.

Jim can be mean, but he's not a bad guy, Blue insisted softly. *Let him help.*

Rin sighed, but he couldn't argue with Blue.

"Let me make up the guest bedroom," Mama insisted, her voice moving farther away from the kitchen as she headed deeper into the house. With any chance of overhearing more of their conversation ended, Rin turned to the beans and started picking.

I am still just as fascinated by you, Blue.

I knew it! Yooouuuu Luuuuvvvv Meeee!

Stop writing in my diary!

No!

*

Jim was already sitting at the breakfast table when Rin and Blue made it downstairs the next morning. Mama had pounded on their bedroom door first thing, then yelled through the bathroom door to hurry them up, which had left Rin with blue balls. He was finally beginning to allow himself to think about Blue in a sexual sense without the fear they would end up destroying the wonderful friendship they already had. Instead, Rin was starting to believe taking that next step would only enhance their relationship, and Mama was, probably unconsciously, driving him mad.

She was cooking breakfast at the stove, already dressed in her work uniform, and looked totally innocent, so Rin toned down his glower and tried to enjoy the smell of banana pancakes wafting his way. Mama was filling plates on the counter, so Rin got out silverware and juice glasses for everyone while Blue raided the pantry for the syrup.

"You like pancakes, Blue?" Jim asked curiously.

Much better than cold, slimy fish. Blue happily plunked the bottle of syrup in front of his seat and sat down to wait. *Mama adds fruit and I pour lots of sugar on top.*

"And then he spends the day galloping around the farm because he's sugar-high," Rin finished with a grin.

Mama brought all four plates over to the table. Blue took his syrup first, pouring until there was more syrup than pancake on his plate. Rin waited until Jim and Mama had taken some before drowning his own pancakes.

"He learned from you," Mama sighed as she looked at Rin's plate. "Anyway, today's chores. First, clean up breakfast. Then I need Tildie and Mary brought back out to the pasture and Demon brought into the empty paddock. Tildie and Mary's paddock needs to be rolled flat again and Demon's stall in the barn cleaned. Only once all those chores are finished can you go swimming," she finished sternly, mostly to Blue, although Rin had been known to abscond with Blue to the lake on occasion.

"Yes, Mama," Rin replied when she waited impatiently for an answer.

Blue snorted but nodded. *Okay. We'll swim later!*

Rin only had a week of freedom left for swimming before his seasonal job started. It was six weeks of pure hell, but it brought in enough money that they didn't have to seriously scrimp during the winter. In winter, there were days the roads were so blocked by snow and ice that Mama couldn't get to work, which meant she wouldn't get paid that day. The extra bit Rin brought in made those snow days a little less terrible. He worked as a security guard for the Saratoga Race Course during the six-week racing season at the end of the summer. It was forty-two hours during a six-day week at ten dollars an hour. It was also the only way Rin could think of to return to the track. He couldn't be at Mama's side as she saddled her horses before the race, but working there was pretty close.

With only one day off a week and the fact that he'd need those full twenty-four hours to recover and prepare for the next six days, swimming wasn't possible. Blue knew that, and Mama knew that, which was one of the reasons she wasn't making them roll both paddocks and sweep out the entire barn.

Mama finished her pancakes and put her plate in the sink. "I'm off. I'll see you tonight," she said with a smile for Rin and Blue. She nodded politely to Jim before leaving the kitchen. Her car rumbled to life a few minutes later.

"So, tell me"—Jim leaned back in his chair, watching Blue lick his plate clean, then take Rin's empty but syrup-covered one and lick that too—"how did Lizzy Roark meet up with a sidhe and sire a son?"

Rin scowled at Jim. It was rude to ask questions like that, especially since he had purposefully waited for Mama to leave before asking. Still, this was a good opportunity to find out more about himself. He stood and gathered the dirty dishes before answering.

"What's a sidhe?"

High fairy. Grumpy fairy. Sourpusses. Bleh.

Jim couldn't stop a grin at Blue's words. "Not entirely inaccurate, unfortunately. The fae or faeries, as Blue has so rudely called us, are a multitude. Blue is a type of fae, a kelpie, but because his form and thoughts are mostly animal in nature, he is considered lesser by those in power."

"That's not right," Rin said. Believing that someone was lesser because they were a little different very often led to terrible crimes. He started stacking the dishes in the dishwasher as he listened.

Jim shrugged. "It's how it's been for longer than humans have been living outside of caves. Those who think without the influence of an animal mind and who lack the characteristics of an animal are called sidhe. I'm a sidhe, for example. These days, we have two courts. The court you would classify as good is called seelie, and the bad is unseelie. They're not very different, to be perfectly honest, just two sides of the same coin. The seelie generally have ties with life magic, growing things and the like, while the unseelie specialize in death. It's warped the unseelie," he added with a twist to his lips Rin could only identify as sad disgust. "They learned hate along with all manner of death."

Seelie, unseelie. They're all grouchy and cranky, Blue insisted.

"Yeah, but a seelie won't kill you for being grumpy in return," Jim said pointedly.

Blue snorted and grabbed the syrup bottle off the table to return it to the pantry.

I'm not an animal because I'm a water horse. Stupid sidhe.

"I think swimming with you is amazing," Rin had to say. Blue sounded depressed and hurt. He had to know there were people like Rin and Mama who didn't care that he was different.

Blue let out a happy squeal and came bouncing out of the pantry. He threw his arms around Rin from behind, knocking the pan he was washing out of his hands. It dropped into the sink with a clang. Rin grabbed Blue's hands in his own soapy ones and squeezed back.

Love you, Blue whispered into Rin's neck, his breath puffing against Rin's skin, which made Rin have totally inappropriate thoughts for a moment when Jim was watching and they still had chores to do.

"You too, you silly kelpie. Now let me go so I can finish cleaning up." Rin smiled as Blue slowly stepped away. He finished washing the pan and placed it in the drying rack, then dried his own hands on the dish towel hanging over the oven. "Outside?"

Have to move the silly sisters, Blue agreed, leading the way through the house and out the front door. *And the Demon*, he added with a sigh. *Stupid horsie*.

"Unfortunately, there aren't any stupid horses, just abused ones," Jim explained from behind them as he followed them through the yard and to the paddock. Mary and Tildie whickered and met them at the fence. It looked like Mama had gotten up early to brush Mary and Tildie; their coats were soft and dust free. Blue whinnied softly at them to say hello. "I've long suspected Wesley and Solomon Stables of neglect and abuse, but there are never any overt signs like scars or starvation on their horses. Just a bad attitude bordering on crazy. Demon is a prime example of their work."

Rin rubbed Mary's nose, her skin soft as velvet under his fingers. He agreed with Jim. Mama had helped Wesley Stables before with horses they couldn't control. Yes, racehorses were high-strung, but they were generally nice horses that loved to run. Horses that would attack their jockey or their handler because the horse was apparently perpetually in a bad mood didn't come along often, so Wesley having so many was a big red flag. And Mama probably knew that too. She had signed a contract with a devil by agreeing to take on Demon, but she was desperate, and Wesley had to have known that.

Rin hated the entire situation. They urgently needed the money, but every time he was reminded of the man who had put Demon in their barn, he gritted his teeth. He took a deep breath and let it out, trying to let the soothing feeling of Mary's nose under his hand calm the angry emotions roiling inside, tightening his stomach and chest.

You need to walk, Blue insisted, glancing down at Rin's legs. *I'll deal with Demon.*

Blue wasn't oblivious to the thoughts spinning through Rin's head, but he always managed to keep the important things forefront in his own mind. Rin let the last of his ire fade away, determined to emulate Blue's stoic acceptance of Demon. There wasn't anything either of them could do to change the situation, so they had to make the best of it.

"You're sure?" Rin asked. Rin knew Blue remembered their first year living together when the physical therapy had started paying off and Rin had slowly been able to walk without the braces and crutches. Blue didn't want Rin to backslide any more than Rin did, so every once in a while, he made Rin walk all the way to the lake or to the pasture for additional practice. Rin would never be able to do all the things he could before the accident, but he could run, and he could certainly walk the distance to the lake and back without too much trouble.

Blue nodded and headed toward the barn. Rin had to hurry and get the mares away before Blue muscled Demon outside and Demon saw them. There were dozens of halters inside the tack shed, some in better repair than others. Rin grabbed two of the good ones and hurried back to the paddock.

Mary and Tildie were well trained. They both lowered their heads so Rin could fasten the halters. He hooked a lead onto both and led them out of the paddock and into the yard. It wasn't a long walk to the pasture. The hardest part was knowing that a few years before, Rin would have hopped onto one of the horses and gotten there in five minutes instead of the fifteen it took on foot. He couldn't do that now. The only horse he could ride was Blue, which was a real shame. Rin wouldn't change what he had with Blue now for anything, but he loved to ride, and if he hadn't gotten hurt, maybe he would be racing at Saratoga instead of working there.

Mama wasn't tall, just five foot five, and Rin had no idea how tall his father might have been, but he had turned out short. Perhaps the accident had stunted his growth like Mama believed. Rin had no way of knowing the truth, but he was barely five foot three, extremely short for a guy, and he was also wire thin thanks to all his time running around with Blue and the fact that Mama couldn't afford to overfeed him. He could have been a jockey if he had the strength in his legs to match his frame, although if he had the muscle he would be too heavy, so it was a silly idea to cling to either way.

Besides, if Rin were riding other horses every day, Blue would get jealous, which might end badly for everyone.

So, Rin walked to the pasture. He was slow enough that Mary and Tildie would pause on their leads to grab some grass to munch on as they walked. There would be plenty of that in the pasture too, but they didn't care. The fence eventually came into sight, and Rin hurried to the gate. He unlatched it and swung it open so Mary and Tildie could wander inside. They let Rin remove their halters before hurrying off to find the choicest bit of grass to have for their third breakfast.

The pasture was the largest flat piece of land on the property, and it had a small stream running through it. Mama had chosen to fence it barely a year before the accident, and the pasture was perfect to give her horses some space to run around and actually be horses. Although, back when she'd had dozens of horses, only the mares and the occasional gelding could use it. Stallions would fight if they were together, so Mama had always kept them well apart.

Most racehorses never saw the outside of their barn stall except when they were led outside for training. Mama hated that practice vehemently. She didn't have the space to give every stallion his own pasture, but the mares had been allowed to run, and she'd done what she could for the rest too.

Rin walked down the path toward the farmhouse. There were still chores to do. He shouldn't spend the morning reminiscing, or they would never get the chance to go swimming.

Jim was wandering around the farm muttering to himself when Rin got back. He went in and out of each barn, shed, and paddock at least three times while Rin grabbed the heavy roller from its hook inside one of those sheds and began pushing it through the paddock Mary and Tildie had left churned up. Hoof scars, rabbit holes, and anything else in the ground that might trip up a horse vanished beneath the roller. Demon was sulking in the other paddock. Apparently Blue had given him a talking-to he didn't appreciate. Blue was making unhappy noises from inside the barn. He wasn't a fan of mucking out stalls, but he would do it if it meant Rin was getting the exercise and practice his legs needed.

It didn't take long to finish the paddock. It was large enough for ten horses to peacefully share, but the roller was efficient as Rin pushed it along. He was tired and sweaty by the time he hung the roller back on its hook, but he still grabbed the bag of grass seed lying nearby. He walked up and down the paddock again, gently tossing seed around. He made sure to cover any spots that looked particularly well chewed. Once that was finished, he put away the bag of grass seed and pulled out the hose to water the paddock and get the new grass growing. It was more than Mama had told him to do, but if Rin didn't do it now, Mama would have to do it when she got home from an exhausting day of waitressing. Besides, Blue had already hauled out the mucky hay and was going beyond his own chores by sweeping out the entire barn. Rin could do no less.

Swimming? Blue asked when Rin started winding up the hose. He'd appeared in the barn doorway, looking dusty and hopeful.

"Let me make sure Demon's feed bin is full, and then yes, let's go swimming," Rin agreed.

Blue squealed happily and spun on his heels to go put the broom away. Rin hurried with the hose and went to check Demon's feed.

"You want to come with us?" Rin asked Jim when he poked his head out of one of the sheds to investigate Blue's noise.

"He doesn't let me go into the water," Jim replied with a shrug. "He'd try to eat me, you understand. Blue wouldn't be able to help it. You're special, clearly," he added with a wide grin.

Rin ducked his head, glad he wasn't prone to blushing. Blue came rushing over before Rin had to come up with a reply. He shifted forms and waited impatiently for Rin to climb on, all under the curiously watchful eye of Jim, and then they galloped off to Blue's lake.

Chapter Three

Neither my mama nor my dad were cowboys. Why does Rin begin all his diary entries about his parents like that? My parents were both proper kelpies with a big lake they shared with me when I was still small. There were lots of fish and even the occasional idiot human to munch on, so I guess we were happy.

I'm happy now that I'm living with Rin, but it's a different sort of happy. My parents weren't snacks. Maybe that's how I should start this.

Neither my mama nor my dad were snacks. I didn't want to eat them; they didn't want to eat me, and we were happy in our lake far, far away from my lake now. It was across the ocean, Jim once told me, but the old lake went bad, and I had to move.

Dad got sick first. I remember the months when his skin was green instead of healthy blue and Mama got more and more worried. She left one day to go find a seelie sidhe who might be willing to heal my dad and the lake that had gotten him sick. I guess Mama didn't know that sidhe were grumpy and mean.

For two months before Dad had turned green, humans had been doing work on the far side of the lake. There had been too many humans for Mama and Dad to safely catch and eat, so they left the humans alone. Once the humans had left, Dad had gone to investigate what they had been doing and had come back sick. There was a new pipe, he had told us, and it was dripping yuck and slime. Mama and I stayed away, but it was too late for Dad.

He died while Mama was gone. I was sad, but there wasn't anything I could do. I waited for weeks and weeks, and then I started turning green. The lake was turning sludgy as the pipe continued to drip. Even though I had stayed on the far side of the lake, I started feeling ill.

I didn't want to leave my happy lake, but Dad was dead, the fish were dying, and Mama was still gone. I needed to find her to tell her about Dad and the lake going bad before I got too sick myself.

To this day I still can't believe I left my lake. Most kelpies only leave their lakes to move into another with their most loved ones, like Dad had when he moved into Mama's lake. Jim says that's what saved my life. Breathing in the tainted water and eating the sick fish had been what had gotten me sick, Jim told me, and leaving had given me a chance to get better.

I never found Mama, but she had apparently found Jim and gotten his promise to stop by her lake to pass on the news that she was still searching. When Jim had found the lake dirty and me missing, he had gone searching for me. We eventually found each other, and he brought me across the ocean to a new lake close enough to Underhill he could continue keeping an eye on me while he looked for Mama to tell her about my new lake.

Jim never found Mama either, but he keeps stopping by to see how I'm doing all the time. I think he likes Rin and Rin's mama because he stayed to help with the horses instead of going back Underhill.

I like living with Rin even if I'm out of my lake much more than any kelpie can usually stand. I moved into Rin's lake, his house, and I'm never planning on leaving.

*

Working at the Saratoga Race Course as a security guard was a trial in patience, purposeful ignorance, and plain stubbornness. It certainly wouldn't ever win any awards for best workplace of the Capital Region, which many other businesses in Saratoga Springs, New York, had earned. Rin hated his job, but he also loved it.

He remembered his interview a year ago, when the director of security had asked him about his job requirements, and Rin had told the director about his messed-up legs. Rin had watched as the director added a note to Rin's file about finding him a primarily seated position. On his first day of work a few weeks later, Rin had learned he was on a walking patrol where sitting wasn't allowed, and there was no way he could be switched to a more appropriate spot.

As he walked around the yard, he met patrons who were noisy, drunk, rude, and demanding. They also had a bad habit of stopping Rin to ask where the bathroom was when it was only two feet away and the sign for it was as evident as the nose on Rin's face. However, his route took him to the fenced horse path that cut through the center of the backyard. Every day, Rin got to see the racehorses led down the path before each race. The horses whinnied, stamped, and argued, but they were loud and beautiful. Rin remembered walking at Mama's side down that exact same horse path. She or one of her handlers would be holding the horse Mama had entered into the race. They would go into the paddock to saddle the horse and greet the jockey, and then Mama's horse would go win the race.

Rin relished the chance to relive some of his happiest memories, even as he detested the work he had to do to have that opportunity.

He could come during the season as a patron instead, but he didn't want to waste the money on gas and admission. This way, he at least got paid.

Rin parked the car in the free lot—employees didn't have parking, so he could either pay with the rest of the patrons or hope the free lot still had open space when he arrived—and double-checked the doors were locked before walking across the lot toward Union Avenue. The track itself was across the street. He slipped through the broken fence around the parking lot and jaywalked across the road. It was easiest to sneak in through the service entrance so he didn't have to interact with any lost and confused patrons before his shift started. The security office was tucked away in the most out-of-the-way and inconvenient location as one might find: on a mezzanine halfway between the first floor of the grandstand and the second. Rin said hello to the other guards he recognized from the previous year, slipped around the new guards for this year who had no idea what they were supposed to be doing, and let the sign-in machine scan his fingerprint. He stopped by the gun cage afterward to get outfitted with his walkie-talkie. He first had to convince the woman inside that his post required one before she allowed him to sign one out. Rin made certain it actually worked before he moved away so the next person could get whatever they needed.

Everyone was wearing the same uncomfortable uniform of navy-blue pants, a navy-blue, collared shirt, a navy-blue hat that read Security on the brim, and a shiny badge that somehow still failed to make the uniform look official. Everyone, Rin included, looked like an awkward mishmash of different shades of faded navy in uniforms that added ten pounds to everyone's frames. It was a sad sight, but it made the overpaid higher-ups happy.

"Roll call!" someone yelled from deeper inside the security office. Rin trooped back into the hallway with everyone else. "Make two straight lines," the sergeant who'd yelled added.

It was Sergeant Savern, a stickler for rules without a lick of sense in his head, as Mama would say. Savern liked things done properly, but Rin didn't think Savern truly understood the mechanics of why and how that was accomplished. Still, he was a unionized import from Belmont, one of the two downstate tracks, and therefore got preference and deference at Saratoga that he didn't deserve.

"Button that shirt. Go shine your shoes! When roll call is over, go get a razor from the gun cage. Your facial hair is embarrassing!" Savern walked up and down the line, searching for reasons to yell at the assembled civilian security guard unit. He thankfully missed the fact that one of Rin's regulation-black shoes had a hole he had duct-taped shut. Rin couldn't afford to buy new shoes for a cracked job like this one, not when boots for the farm were much more important, and there were more than enough other places for the money to go.

The captain from the previous year had apparently been made director over the summer, Rin saw as now-Director Summers stepped out of the director's office with a spiffy new hat and a uniform that made him look like he worked for the state police. Rin always wondered why they tried to emulate the police so closely with their civilian force at Saratoga, but it was easy to see Director Summers was reveling in this chance to return to his heyday. Rin could understand that sentiment since he wouldn't be working this particular job if he hadn't wanted the same thing.

"Welcome," Director Summers said after Sergeant Savern had made a formal introduction. "I'm expecting to have a great meet this year, and with your help, we can make that happen! Make sure to speak with your sergeants about how your individual posts work. This year, we're going to emphasize customer service, so make sure you're very welcoming. Smile and listen when a patron asks for help." He continued along that vein for a while more, but Rin tuned him out. It was the same speech the previous director had barked at them last year, but changed enough that Summers probably thought he was being original.

Eventually Savern yelled, "Dismissed!" and Rin headed out of the security office toward his post as the two lines dispersed into a disorganized mass of confusion.

"Patrolman Roark!" Another sergeant Rin didn't recognize, but who apparently knew who Rin was, yelled and waved from farther down the hall. There were other security guards milling around him. Rin frowned and switched directions to walk over there. "I think we're all here," the sergeant continued gamely when Rin reached him. "Welcome to sector seven. I'm Sergeant Freed. Our duty is primarily the horse path, which includes much of the backyard and the Big Red Spring. I'll be assigning your posts now. Any questions?"

Rin raised his hand. "I'm sector seven, post thirteen," he said when Freed looked at him. "Do you want me to wait until you're done here, or go assume my post now?"

"Post thirteen, post thirteen," Freed mumbled under his breath as he flipped through a stack of papers in his hand. He pulled out one sheet near the bottom and read through it. "Thirteen is on patrol in the yard from the Big Red Spring to the playground with occasional help in the paddock during big races," he read. "Is that the post you want? I was thinking of putting you on the horse path itself, near Gate B."

"I had post thirteen last year and I would like to have it again." The last thing he wanted was to get stuck on the horse path, a position where he would have to stand in exactly one spot—except when any horses came up the path, at which point he would have to pull a dirty chain across the pedestrian portion of the path to keep the idiot patrons from meeting up with an irate horse. It was one of the worst positions on the track.

"I suppose if that's what you want," Freed said, sounding extremely reluctant. He slowly held out the paper in his hand for Rin to take. Rin didn't miss his sidelong glance at another man standing nearby, and suddenly Rin understood what he had gotten in the middle of. Both men had to be from downstate. One was a sergeant who had pulled strings to get his friend placed in his sector. Giving his friend Rin's roaming position meant they could both wander around together. Having someone to talk to during the long day was nice, so Rin did understand, but he had seen this sort of thing happen last year in the jockey escorts, sector four, and knew it was essentially a way for the unionized downstaters to skive off work without appearing to be doing exactly that.

He took the piece of paper with his post's description on it from Freed before Freed could change his mind.

"I'll be down to check on you," Freed said in dismissal.

Rin left immediately to keep the situation from escalating. Given a few days, the problem would take care of itself. Freed would manufacture a new roaming position for his friend, so he would still get what he wanted and none of the higher-ups would dare to stop him because he was unionized, and no one wanted to fight against the union.

Rin returned to the first floor and shook himself out of his thoughts. It was only eleven thirty and the first race wouldn't go off until one o'clock, but patrons were already filling the grounds. He crossed the horse path at the Gate B intersection, glad yet again he wasn't stuck there for the entire summer, and headed toward the Big Red Spring—one of the sulfur springs that had given Saratoga Springs its name—in the far corner.

Rin's route was simple. He started at the Big Red Spring, walked along the fence line of the paddock, and followed the fence outside of the horse path until he reached Gate A, which was near the security office. His job was to ensure no one was placing their tents or umbrellas too close to the fence in order to keep loose or flapping fabric from scaring the horses as they walked by. He followed the sidewalk that cut through the middle of the yard parallel to the horse path on his way back. It took him past the large mutual bay between Gates A and B, where he checked in with the guard stationed on the chair outside the bay door, and past two smaller mutual bays closer to the Big Red Spring, again checking in with the guard sitting outside of those bays.

That was his day. For seven hours he walked that circle, only pausing to give patrons directions or to correct a misplaced tent. Midway through the day, he had an hour for his lunch, which he ate in a tiny back room near the security office that had somehow been dubbed the security break room even though every employee on the track had access to it. Eight hours after he had scanned his finger to sign in, Rin scanned his finger to sign out. His feet ached, his legs ached, and his head ached as he left through the service entrance. He jaywalked across Union Avenue, took the shortcut through the broken fence, and found his car for the twenty-minute drive home.

*

Blue galloped along the drive as Rin drove the last few yards to the house and parked next to Mama's car. Blue shifted into human form as Rin slowly and stiffly got out of the car. He grabbed Rin and yanked him into a hug.

Mama says take a hot bath. Dinner will be ready soon. Before Rin could answer, Blue dragged him into the house and up the stairs. Blue got distracted with turning on the tap and making sure the water was the right temperature, which gave Rin a moment to get his shoes off and to start peeling himself out of his uniform.

The tub filled quickly, steam rising into the air. Blue waited expectantly, sitting on the floor next to the tub, for Rin to get in. Last year, Blue had been willing to stay with Mama to help with dinner while Rin washed off the stench of the track. Apparently, enough had changed in their relationship that Blue wasn't going to leave. It was too bad Rin was too tired to take advantage of the situation, what with Mama distracted downstairs and Blue waiting happily for him to strip naked.

His tired fingers fumbled with the buttons of his shirt as he slowly took all of his clothes off and stepped into the tub. The water was warm, and Rin groaned as he finally took his weight off his feet and the heat sank into aching muscles. Blue reached across Rin's body and grabbed the body wash. He dunked a washcloth into the water and squeezed some soap onto it and rubbed the cloth together to make a lather.

Lean forward, Blue instructed.

Rin complied, and the washcloth brushed down his back. Blue rumbled happily as he finished Rin's back and moved on down his arms. Rin had thought he was too tired for any fun a moment ago, but the feel of Blue's warm hands combined with the comfort of the water had him getting hard.

Blue hummed softly and leaned his head against Rin's shoulder as his hand drifted from Rin's arm to his chest and farther down.

You're a delicious snack, Blue whispered. He tilted his head to nibble lightly on Rin's neck as he dropped the washcloth into the water and grabbed Rin's length in a firm grip. Rin groaned and tilted his head to the side to give Blue's teeth better access at the same time as his hips arched involuntarily upward. Water sloshed around him as Blue's humming grew louder along with the pace his fist was moving.

They had never touched like this before. Awkward fumbling in the dark of night or first thing in the morning before Mama knocked had never led to skin touching skin or Blue's breath in Rin's ear as they both panted and groaned.

With Blue's hand stroking him and Blue's teeth in Rin's neck, Rin couldn't help whimpering and coming hard. The water calmed around them as Rin panted and his heart rate slowed. Blue's head was resting on Rin's shoulder, his teeth thankfully no longer in Rin's skin. Rin tilted his head slightly, forcing Blue to look up, and pressed his lips against Blue's.

Blue rumbled deep in his throat, a sort of purring sound Rin only heard when Blue was particularly happy. Rin pulled away slowly, his lips wet and aching from the kiss.

"I guess I should finish cleaning up," Rin said, his voice deeper than normal as he stared into Blue's wide eyes.

I have to change my pants, Blue grumbled. *Next time I'm going to eat you while we're in the bath together.*

Rin laughed as Blue stood and pawed disgustedly at the damp spot on the front of his pants. "I'll finish washing. You go get changed, and we'll both help Mama with dinner."

I'm hungry, Blue agreed. *You're a satisfying snack, but you fill things other than my stomach.*

"Right here?" Rin asked hopefully, placing his hand over his heart.

Duh. Hurry up. Mama's making steak!

Blue left the bathroom in search of clean pants while Rin reached forward to unplug the drain. The water was gross from the dirt of the day and from coming in it. He let it all drain out and turned on the shower to finish getting clean. Blue continued humming happily in Rin's head as he quickly scrubbed and rinsed, and then he met Rin at Rin's bedroom door with a pair of clean pajama pants.

He was feeling shameless, Rin decided. He and Blue had finally done something sexual in their relationship, and they weren't going to change in any way because of it. There was a new dimension, but Blue was still Blue, and Rin still loved Blue for that.

Rin let his towel drop to the floor as he took the pajamas from Blue, who grinned and whickered at the sight before leaning forward to briefly press his lips against Rin's.

I like kissing too. We'll have to do that a lot!

Rin had no issues with that. He yanked on the pants, and then leaned forward to take a longer and much more involved kiss from Blue. Rin was half-hard again when he pulled away, but he knew Mama's lack of yelling at him to help get dinner ready was a very temporary thing. He didn't have time at the moment to do everything he wanted with Blue, but once Mama was in bed across the house, there would be plenty of opportunity.

"Let's go have dinner," he said, taking Blue's hand in his and pulling him out of the room and down the stairs.

"Just let me help, Lizzy," Jim was saying as they approached the kitchen. Rin couldn't help freezing outside the kitchen door to overhear more. "You've at least one shed that's rotted through and won't last the winter, and you've barely got enough hay stockpiled for the rest of the summer. You'll be paying through the nose in March to get feed for your three horses. I'm not talking about a lot of money; a small loan to get you through the next three or so years. You'll pay me back as soon as you start winning stakes races again."

"I've managed this far on my own, and I can keep on doing it," Mama insisted stubbornly.

"But you don't have to," Jim replied equally as stubbornly. "It's not charity, just good business. If you're too focused on rebuilding your stable, how can you properly look after the horses in your barn?"

"I'll think about it," Mama said with a tone of finality. She was done talking about it, at least. Whether she would actually think about it was another matter entirely. "Stop hovering outside the door, boys," she added sharply. "The table isn't going to set itself."

How do you help your family, your most precious snack, when you know they are hurting? I know you don't have any answers, Rin's journal, but I didn't either. I didn't even know what a house was until my snack explained that the building with all of its rooms and such was his equivalent to my lake. You can't swim in the house—even the bathtub is too small for that—but it's still a comfortable, wonderful place to live.

I'm good at sneaking around and reading stuff I'm not supposed to. Rin, I know you'll roll your eyes when you read that since I'm writing in your journal again, but I am. I know what it means when Mama's letters are threatening to repossess the house, the car, or the horses. It means the lake will be gone, and Rin will be forced to wander the wilderness until someone like Jim takes him in and helps him find a new lake.

I would follow you on that journey, Rin, but it's not something you or I want to have to do. But what could I do to stop it from happening? I hoped Jim would have some funds to help, so I asked him. I knew if he came here and met my family, he would help them like he had helped me. Well, once he gets past Mama being stubborn, of course.

So, no, I didn't forget sending Jim that letter. My pretty snack, will you forgive me for that? I can't lose another lake or another family, and this will solve everything. I just know it will!

You're off at work now, doing everything you can to help out. Mama's working too, and Jim was busy scowling outside Demon's paddock. I admit, I'm a little bored and lonely sitting here on my own, writing serious and sad things in a book because saying them aloud is so much harder. It would be better if my snack were here with me, keeping the boredom away. Being bored isn't very fun.

Jim says I should practice my glamor to fill my spare time, that I shouldn't have horns or blue lips in human form and that I don't look very horselike when I'm in horse form. I'm around humans, he explained, so I should look more normal to them. But my snack likes my horns!

But there is somewhere I can go where I'll be practicing my glamor, and I'll get to see you, my pretty snack! Maybe I can apologize for lying to you, and I won't be bored too.

*

"Hey, mister! Is the ghost going to be around this season?"

Rin turned around, automatically plastering a smile on his face. There were three people standing there. They looked like a small family: mom, dad, and little girl. The girl was clutching a plastic bucket to her chest. Rin could see cucumbers inside and fought not to roll his eyes and offend the family. Freed had echoed Director Summers's customer-service-is-the-top-priority speech this morning when he'd met with sector seven, and Rin didn't want to get in trouble for ignoring that policy so early in the meet. The downstaters were the only ones who could get away with that with impunity.

It was the dad who had so rudely spoken, but Rin knelt onto one knee to speak with the girl. "The ghost hasn't been seen yet," Rin answered, "but it's still early in the meet. I'll bet he'll show up soon."

"Damned publicity stunt," the dad muttered under his breath. If it was a publicity stunt put on by the track, it had clearly worked because the family had come. The ghost wasn't a stunt, although Rin was one of the very few people who knew that for certain.

"Really?" the girl asked with a gap-toothed grin. "I brought him a treat!" She held out the bucket for Rin to see. There was a lone carrot at the bottom, probably an addition by a parent who doubted the magical ghost horse who had appeared at the track last season would eat cucumbers.

"I can't promise that he'll show up today," Rin said, "but if he does, he'll love eating your snack."

"I knew it," the girl said with a wide grin up at her mother. Her dad rolled his eyes, but they all wandered off happy without a word of thanks to Rin. They saw his uniform, as ill-fitting as it was, more clearly than the man wearing it. That was what the track wanted, of course: a unified force where the roles of the individuals who comprised it were the same, while the faces of its makeup were interchangeable. That was the way the track worked, and Rin had learned to live with it.

He continued along his route, pointing out bathrooms and mutual bays to oblivious patrons as he went. The worst security problem he had ever encountered was a missing family member, but the track was very proud of their statistic of never losing someone permanently. Lost children and grandparents were always eventually found. His radio crackled almost constantly with what other patrolmen and women were doing around the track. There were a lot of money escorts needed today, his radio informed him over and over again.

Another hour passed uneventfully. Despite its monotony, he earned ten dollars—minus taxes—for doing almost nothing. He really shouldn't complain. The horses for the races went by twice in that hour, once when he was patrolling along the horse path, so he got to see them closely. The races weren't stakes races, and the horses weren't spectacular-looking like a horse running in a Grade I would be, but it was exciting to see all the same. It was why he had taken this job, after all. He had even discreetly paused near one of the TV stands to watch a couple of races. He wasn't supposed to be so derelict in his duties, but Rin couldn't help watching anyway.

A glance at his watch told him he still had another forty-five minutes before his relief came to give him his hour break. His stomach was beginning to rumble, and he thought fondly of the chicken salad sandwich Mama had made him with the leftovers from dinner.

"Patrolman Jack to the security desk," Rin's radio squawked.

"This is the security desk," a second voice squawked.

"There appears to be a...um...blue horse? A loose horse swimming in the infield pond," Patrolman Jack said hesitantly.

Rin sighed and rolled his eyes. Blue's presence at the track was inevitable. When he had done this last year, he had caused so much drama in the security office. At least the rest of the day would be more interesting. Rin could practically hear them swearing in the security office. Unfortunately, they were smart enough not to broadcast it. He could've used a good laugh.

"Keep an eye on that horse if you're able to, Patrolman Jack. Lieutenant Cristobel will meet with you to assess the situation."

"Ten-four!" Patrolman Jack replied. "Ten-four" in security guard terms was stupid speak for someone too hopped up on the power of their badge to simply say they understood. For actual sworn-in policemen and military personnel, it meant that, but a security guard was a civilian handed a badge. All too often that façade of power went to people's heads. Rin had seen it happen very frequently at the track. Every once in a while, he heard stories about guards caught patrolling with nunchucks or something else idiotic and getting fired, but that was an extreme case. Most of the hopped-up guards bought themselves big belts they could hang a dozen "useful" gadgets from. It usually ended up being an empty mace holder, an empty handcuffs holder, and so on because ordinary security guards weren't allowed to carry that sort of stuff. Rin rolled his eyes whenever he saw it, but it was funny enough that it helped keep the day moving.

Rin continued walking for a few more minutes, and thankfully, the walkie-talkie didn't squawk in his ear.

Patrolmen like Rin were told to never, ever be on their cell phones, yet the security desk preferred the patrolmen call via cell phone instead of radio. It left the radio open in case of a real emergency. The desk was probably confirming Patrolman Jack's location that way.

Blue would be long gone by the time anyone reached Jack, so he wasn't worried; Blue knew better than to eat someone where Rin might find out about it. There was no way Rin would respect Blue if he knew Blue had eaten someone while living in Mama's house, and Blue definitely knew that. It was a firm discussion they'd had last year when Blue had first shown up at the track. Besides, there were always cucumbers to eat if Blue got hungry, and that was almost as good to Blue.

The horses for the next race were being led along the horse path and into the paddock as Rin walked by, so he paused to look. There was a brown mare Rin liked the look of. Her hot walker, a surly-looking Hispanic man, was wearing the six jersey. She looked eager and happy. Her eyes were bright, her steps high, and her muscles sleek. It wouldn't surprise Rin if she won the race. There were always other factors at play in a race though. The ability of the jockey, the state of the track itself, and whether the horse actually felt like running that day all played into the eventual outcome. He had seen races when a favorite refused to break from the gate entirely.

"Patrolman Arnold, Patrolman Griggs, Patrolwoman Morales, and Patrolman Roark," the radio squawked. "Report to Lieutenant Cristobel at the top of the stretch."

Three different versions of "ten-four" sounded from the radio. Rin hit the button to reply and said, "Patrolman Roark confirms." He took the sidewalk that ran parallel to the horse path so he could stop by the two seated guards at the mutual bays to warn them he had been called away. They didn't merit radios, although that was most likely because the track simply didn't have enough to give them.

As the horses ran around the track, they passed the top of the stretch, or the final turn, as they headed toward the finish line. Saratoga had created a picnic area there as part of the grandstand seating—first come, first served, and Rin never wanted to be there first thing in the morning when patrons were rushing to get the picnic benches along the rail. It was also next to the service entrance Rin used to get into the security office in the morning. Either Lieutenant Cristobel hadn't wanted to bother walking all the way to the finish line, which was the best place to cross the rail and get onto the track, but was also a long walk from the security office, or Patrolman Jack was stationed there. Rin felt sorry for the poor guy if that was the case.

He made his way to the group of guards forming around the man wearing the white uniform shirt, an honor given only to lieutenants and up.

"Listen up," Lieutenant Cristobel said once everyone was present. "We think it's the same horse as last year. It can't get out of the track without help, so we're going to corner it for the outrider to catch." An outrider was the horse and rider who helped keep the racehorses in line before and after a race. If a horse escaped its handler or jockey, the outriders were supposed to catch it. What Cristobel hadn't mentioned was how the mystery horse had gotten onto the infield in the first place, given the space was completely enclosed. The little girl from earlier in the day hadn't been wrong in calling "it" a ghost.

An average patron could not access the track and the infield where the lake was. The track was surrounded by a safety fence. Outside that fence were the grandstand and clubhouse on one side of the track, and the far side had the barns. There were three entrances for horses: one near the top of the stretch and one by the barns—both of which were locked during the races and opened to let the tired horses out when the race was complete—and the last was the entrance for the horse path that was mostly used during the races themselves. The only entrance that was unlocked for people to get onto the track was in the winner's circle at the finish line, and just the horse owners, trainers, and hot walkers were allowed that privilege. Every entrance was watched closely by security, and it was inconceivable that a horse could sneak through.

Of course, security just didn't have the ability to account for someone like Blue.

Rin and his fellow patrolmen were being sent on a wild goose chase. At least it broke up the monotony of the day, but Rin was going to be late for his lunch hour because of this.

"I'm waiting on confirmation that the horses for the next race are going to be held in the paddock until we clear the infield," Cristobel finished. They waited for a few more minutes, more than enough time for the horses to come out from the paddock saddled and with their jockeys onboard. Since the bugler didn't sound the call to post, Rin felt it was safe to assume Cristobel could use the key he was holding to open the padlock on the gate and let them onto the track.

Finally, Cristobel's cell phone buzzed from where it was hanging in a case on his belt. Cristobel answered curtly and listened for a few long moments. His face was getting cloudier the longer the person on the other end spoke. He hung up and swore loudly, attracting quite a few alarmed stares from the patrons nearby.

"The damned ghost has vanished," he snarled. "The outriders swept the infield a second time, and now they can't find any sign of him. The bigwigs want to go ahead with the race. Head back to your posts, but keep an eye out for that damned horse."

He strode away, heading toward the security office as the bugler began to play and the horses began to appear on the track. Rin shared a wide-eyed look with the other patrolmen, but no one wanted to stick around to gossip and get yelled at. Rin was the only one heading through the grandstand and out into the yard. He passed the stairs to the security office, then crossed the horse path at Gate A and resumed his route.

Two minutes later, a blue horse trotted past him, a very familiar little girl's bucket hanging between his teeth. He vanished behind the large mutual bay between Gate A and Gate B. Rin followed, but he circled the bay twice and didn't see any sign of Blue.

For the next half hour, the radio squawked almost constantly as sighting after sighting was reported. The girl who did reliefs appeared exactly on time, and Rin was glad to hand over his radio to her.

"See you in an hour," he said, wondering if she had ever told him her name.

"Have a good lunch," she replied absentmindedly. She was craning her neck to look around, no doubt hoping to see the ghost horse. Rin wished her luck a touch too sarcastically in his head as he headed toward the security break room where his lunch was waiting.

When Rin's hour was over, he packed up what was left of his lunch and headed outside. Blue was waiting at the foot of the stairs in his human form, grinning widely up at Rin as Rin descended.

"You cause so many problems," Rin couldn't help saying. He was smiling as he spoke though. Seeing Blue was always welcome, and Blue's hijinks did help to break the monotony of Rin's day. It also made Rin's coworkers actually have to do work, which was a nice change too.

Blue whickered lightly under his breath. *I was bored. Now I'm not.*

Rin's smile widened, and he stepped forward to pull Blue into a hug. "We can't have that," he murmured into Blue's ear.

"Roark! Get back on your post!" Sergeant Freed stomped up to him, a disgusted sneer firmly plastered on his face. "You can fraternize with your boyfriend on your own time." Rin stepped away from Blue, although he didn't go far. If Freed had a problem with Rin being gay, he could stuff himself. A glance at Rin's watch told him he still had five minutes before he needed to be back on his post, not that Freed had bothered to learn something as important as his patrolmen's break hours.

"I'll see you at home?" Rin asked Blue. He hadn't turned his back on Freed—he didn't want to appear to be ignoring his sergeant—but at the same time, he wasn't about to lose his five minutes. Especially since those minutes were with Blue, and Rin wasn't getting paid for them. His hour off was his own time, unpaid, and Freed wasn't taking any of that from him.

Blue grinned, then turned and trotted off. Rin nodded to Freed, who was still scowling at him, and went to let his relief move on to her next position.

*

Rin held back a yawn as he parked his car next to Mama's on the drive. He pulled the key and climbed out onto the hard-packed dirt of the yard. Blue was lying in the empty paddock, curled up in his most horselike form and napping in the sun. He opened one eye when Rin walked over to the fence.

I did too much today. Even Blue's voice sounded sleepy. *Go have a bath, and come nap with me.*

Rin laughed. He was tired too, his legs aching from all the walking. It was a good ache, though, that spoke of well-worked muscles, not injured ones. There would always be metal holding his bones together, but he was healed enough to appreciate how his legs felt now.

It didn't take long to shower and get dressed in something loose and comfortable. Blue hadn't moved from the paddock in the interim, but a strange car pulled up the drive as Rin stepped outside to go curl up with Blue.

James Wesley was easily recognizable. His hair was bleached platinum blond, but his goatee was still dark brown. Both his ears were pierced, and heavy diamond studs hung from the lobes. He was wearing an expensive suit despite the heat of the afternoon and the fact that he was walking onto a dirty farm.

Rin remembered him mostly from the days when Mama still raced her horses. There were the horses she had managed to gentle for him, plus all the races where her own horses had beat his to the finish line easily. His smile had always been false and touched with Botox, and he hadn't changed in the years since.

Wesley strode across the yard toward Rin, who had paused halfway out the front door, but he stopped short midway and turned to face Blue in the paddock. He stomped over to the fence and swore loudly when he got a good look at Blue.

"I knew it! I knew it!" he yelled, whirling to face the house again. "I knew you were cheating me!"

Mama came up behind Rin and gently pulled him aside so she could get around him. Jim appeared at the entrance to the empty barn, a frown on his dark face.

"Cheating you?" Mama asked sharply, stepping out into the yard.

"That right there is a blue yearling, clearly one of Demon's get," Wesley hissed, his face stiff from too many surgeries for his mouth to turn into a proper, glowering frown. He looked comical, but Rin didn't feel like laughing. "I knew something was going on when I saw the sudden influx of blue roan colts and fillies hitting the markets lately. I told myself, no, Lizzy wouldn't do that to me, but it turns out I was wrong. You had a foal off him in the first week and have been selling them for profit, all while telling me Demon wasn't ready yet."

Mama was gaping at him, her mouth hanging slightly open in shock even as anger stiffened her spine. Blue hadn't bothered to pay attention before, but he jumped to his feet with a whinny at Wesley's loud exclamation. Blue's glamor was perfect, his coat believably shaded with no evidence of horns or pointed ears, but the fire in his eyes was pure malice.

I'm going to eat him, Blue growled. He stalked forward through the paddock, only to freeze in place when Jim jumped the paddock fence and hurried over to drop a heavy hand on his shoulder.

"Was this your scheme all along?" Jim asked. His eyes were cold and hard, but they were human-looking. With his glamor in place, his skin, eyes, and hair were a dark shade of brown. The points to his ears were gone too. That didn't stop him from looking dangerous as he left Blue and walked to the fence that separated him from Wesley.

While Jim outwardly looked calm—albeit definitely still angry—something in Jim's voice had Rin wanting to take a step back. Jim had a dark sibilant hissing tone that said he knew how to hunt and how to kill, and that the human standing in front of him would be perfect prey. A punch of fear hit Rin in the chest, making his lungs and stomach clench until it was hard to breathe, and all he wanted to do was curl up into a ball and hide until the danger had passed.

"Let Lizzy Roark do all the hard work," Jim continued, and Rin had to lock his knees to keep from running into the house where he would be safe. "After an appropriate amount of time, you planned to accuse her of defrauding you so you could reap the benefits without having to pay for her services?"

"Jim O'Malley?" Wesley said. His voice and stance had turned from aggressive to scared the second Jim had spoken. His back curled slightly, and he shuffled his expensively clad feet in the dirt as he stepped away toward his car.

"I think you need to get in your car and drive home. Shelve your scheme, and as an act of goodwill, I think you should let Lizzy have Demon and the colt."

Some of Wesley's spine resurged as his back hit the apparently steadying metal of his car door. "My lawyer will be by with paperwork in a few hours, Elizabeth Roark. I'll have your entire farm for this!"

Those words were almost scarier than Jim's. Mama didn't have the money or the clout to fight even so weak a threat. They would lose their house and the horses, and the gleeful glint in Wesley's eyes said he knew that perfectly well. He had backed them into a corner, which left them with two options—only one of which Wesley was aware of. They could either give Wesley everything he wanted, or Mama could accept Jim's money. The first would ruin them as thoroughly as a legal battle; the second would neatly indebt them to Jim, who claimed he only wanted to help. Rin wasn't so sure that was Jim's only motive, but now wasn't the time to dwell on that. Thankfully, with his last words still hovering in the air, Wesley got into his car and sped off down the driveway with a spray of dirt as his tires spun for a moment.

"I could have handled him without your help," Mama said. Some of the anger tightening her voice was left over from Wesley, but Mama was an independent woman who had never appreciated a man telling her what to do. She didn't seem to be the least bit affected by Jim, but Rin had to take a few deep breaths and steady himself against the jamb for a long second before the fear began to dissipate and strength returned to his legs.

Jim just grinned in response. "I know you could have, but Blue would have finished it for you."

Mama frowned over at Blue. "If you live in my house, you won't be eating any humans," she scolded.

Blue let out a snort as his form shimmered and his human body replaced the horse. He still nodded to Mama to show he understood her before hopping over the paddock fence and hurrying to where Rin remained, hovering in the open doorway.

"What if he does sue us, Mama?" Rin had to ask. His voice was soft and shaky as the reality of their situation set in. They couldn't afford a lawyer to fight off Wesley's claim. They could lose all their horses, the farm, and their house to Wesley's greed.

"One day I'm going to catch that bastard milkshaking, and no one will have to worry about trying to keep a step ahead of his cheating," Jim grumbled. "The way I see it, I need to have someone look into where all these alleged blue roans in the market are coming from. If I can trace them to Wesley and Solomon, any lawsuit he comes up with will get dropped in a hoofbeat. But I have to admit he might have given us both a solution to our problems."

This time Mama let out an angry snort of disbelief. She quickly covered her mouth and nose with a hand as if to say a lady wouldn't have made that type of sound. It was another holdover from her childhood, Rin knew, and it made Jim's grin grow slightly. Rin wasn't exactly certain he liked where Jim and Mama's relationship appeared to be going. A very large part of him wanted to step in between them so he could glare at Jim.

The other, smaller part won by reminding him Mama might enjoy meddling with Rin and Blue, but she had never outright done anything to forbid their relationship. Rin didn't have to like Jim and Mama sharing a smile, but he would let her get on with it. And then he and Blue would kill Jim the second he hurt Mama.

"What's your idea?" Rin asked, trying to refocus himself on the more important issue.

This time Jim's grin wasn't at all friendly. It had an edge to it Rin usually only saw when Blue flashed his pointed teeth.

"We can pretend Lizzy contracted with me at the same time as Wesley. After all, to the rest of the world, Jim O'Malley is reaching fifty years old. It's not inconceivable a man of my alleged age would look for help with his own recalcitrant horses, and Lizzy is the best in the business. Lizzy, you were merely diversifying your opportunities to get back into the game, and unlike with Demon, you were immediately successful with the stallion I brought you. I say we pretend Blue is the result of one of mine and one of yours, and have Blue run at least one or two races this season. He'll look the part if Wesley is correct and there are an increased number of blue horses on the market. No one will remark on the oddity of it.

"It'll get your name back in the spotlight," he added to Mama. "People will see you and remember how honorable you were, which will help deflect some of the vitriol Wesley will be spewing. Blue will win his races, which will bring in enough money into the farm to make the repairs you need. That way you won't have to borrow any money from me to restart your breeding and training program."

"I'll still be using your horses," Mama pointed out. "And I didn't think you had a blue stallion in your stables to pass on those traits to Blue."

"Think of using my horses like a breeding fee from me. Instead of my paying you money for each resulting foal, you'll keep the foal. It's about even in the end, and soon enough you'll have enough horses that are outright yours you won't need any of mine anymore. As for the blue sire, I do have a black stallion I always felt was too flighty to race. I was thinking about breeding him if I found the right mare. It wouldn't be hard for me to change his paperwork to say he's a blue roan darkened with age."

It all sounded like a good idea to Rin. "Get your horses back on the track, Mama, and you'll win races again. The money will come back; you can quit your waitressing job and start buying new breeding stock for even better horses."

"Mary and Tildie are the two best results from before," Mama said softly. "With them, another stallion, and a few of your mares for breeding stock, I could do it. And imagine if I could keep Demon too!"

Blue had his arm wrapped around Rin's waist, but he hadn't added anything to the conversation. Rin looked up at Blue, who was frowning.

"Do you want to do it?" Rin asked softly. He turned so he could wrap both his arms around Blue's middle in a loose hug. The entire plan hinged on Blue, but no one had even asked Blue what he wanted.

It'll help Mama, Blue replied hesitantly. *But I'm better at swimming than running.*

"I can teach you. Teach you both, actually." Jim looked at Rin thoughtfully, then glanced sidelong at Mama, who grinned conspiratorially with him.

"Both?" Rin asked.

Jim nodded. "Have you ever wanted to be a jockey, Rin?"

Chapter Four

Sitting on Blue's back had never been a hardship for Rin. The feel of Blue's soft fur over hard muscle and bone was almost as interesting as when Blue lay over Rin while they were sleeping. This time, however, the hard press of stiffened leather separated them. Rin couldn't say he liked that feeling, and Blue didn't exactly enjoy having a saddle tied to his back either.

"Again!" Jim called.

Blue let out a grumbling whinny, but he obediently stepped into position at their improvised starting line. Rin took a few extra seconds to situate himself. He knew how to ride a horse, but riding as a jockey was different. He essentially crouched in the saddle with his head low over Blue's neck to reduce wind resistance, and his knees bent so they could flex with the up-and-down movement of Blue's stride. It wasn't a comfortable position to be in at all.

Rin had seen plenty of jockeys do this before—at the track and here at the farm. They used to come by a couple of days before races to take a few test laps and get a feel for a horse. Some had even been riders for Mama in the off-season. None of them had seemed to have the same trouble Rin was having, but then, none of them had stopped riding almost entirely for a few years.

We've got this, Rin, Blue said comfortingly. His voice sounded as tired as Rin felt—slightly beat-up and scratchy—but he was willing to give it another try, so Rin needed to try too.

He got his body into the proper stance, and Jim yelled "Go!" Blue took off, and Rin immediately fought to keep his butt off the saddle. He locked his knees in place, leaned forward over Blue's back, and Blue ran in a wide circle around the paddock. They made it twice around before Rin's legs gave out, and he collapsed backward onto the saddle. He would have kept sliding off the thin leather, but the welcome tingle of Blue's magic snapped into place before that could happen.

We did good this time! Blue crowed happily. *We got around twice.*

And despite the aches in his legs, Rin had managed to stay in place. "We did do good this time," Rin replied in agreement. They both turned to look at Jim, who nodded at them.

"We're done for today. Go shower and get ready for dinner. I'll clean up out here." Jim waved them toward the open gate, and Blue didn't waste any time heading into the yard. Rin had to wait a moment for Blue's magic to fade before he carefully slid off Blue's back. He was quick to unhook the saddle and bitless bridle, and when Jim pointed, he laid them over the fence.

"We're pretty good at this," Rin said to Blue as Blue's form shimmered, and his horse form was replaced with his human form. They headed into the house together, where they were greeted by the scent of some sort of meat cooking. Mama would yell if they tried to go into the kitchen to wait for dinner while smelling as rank as they did, so they headed upstairs for a shower first.

Swimming's still more fun, Blue replied grumpily, but he grinned at Rin a second later. *I don't mind as long as it's you on my back, and it'll help Mama. One race to save the farm, and we can swim after.*

Rin couldn't help smiling back, but then they started taking off their sweaty clothes as the water began to warm in the shower, and their excitement over beginning to figure racing out turned into a different sort of excitement entirely.

*

One week later, they were out in the far pasture to train. There was so much more room to run, and Mary and Tildie didn't mind the company. They continued to crop grass in the middle of the wide space even as Blue was running around them.

Blue was doing so much more work than Rin, who had to spend six days a week at his job and could only work with Blue in the evenings and on his lone day off. Rin would hurry home every afternoon aching from a long day walking in circles and pointing drunken patrons in the direction of the nearest bathroom, only to find an equally exhausted Blue had spent the day running in circles too.

There was a lot to Blue's running though. First, he had to stay in horse form without any evidence of his horns or pointed teeth. Plus, Jim was having Blue tone down the shade of his coat to look a little more normal, which Blue was finding particularly difficult. Never before in his life had Blue needed to perfect his glamor to such an extent. Doing it while running wasn't easy.

It was only on days when Jim had something else he needed to do that Blue had been able to sneak away to terrorize the security guards at the track. Listening to the mostly inane panic on Rin's walkie-talkie combined with the excitement of the patrons made the last few hours of his shifts practically fly by. He would then return home, sometimes with Blue in his passenger seat, and Jim would descend on them.

Over the past week, Blue had been able to sneak away twice, and Jim had declared they were both proficient enough to move out to the far pasture.

"You're going to be put into a starting gate," Jim explained as Rin and Blue rested after yet another run around the pasture. Rin was still sitting on Blue's back, but he had his chest resting on Blue's long neck and his arms wrapped around Blue in a hug. "It's a tight fit, so it will feel a bit uncomfortable, but that's how the races begin, so you'll both have to live with it. Once all the horses are situated, the gates will pop open, and you'll have to sprint out of the gate to get in front of all the other horses who will be doing the same."

"We should stay in front of the herd?" Rin asked. Blue was faster than a regular horse thanks to his magic, so Rin thought it might be better to stay in the middle of the pack where Blue could pace himself easier.

I've been working on running slow while not looking like it, Blue explained.

"It would be better to stay in front," Jim added. "There's too much bumping and jostling in the middle of the pack, and trying to win from the rear might mean Blue has to resort to too much speed."

Rin knew what Jim wasn't saying. Blue was more than strong enough to withstand the bumping and shoving, but one hit would no doubt send Rin flying. His weakness was causing Blue to have to work so much harder.

His arms must have involuntarily tightened around Blue at that thought because Blue whickered at him gently. *It's not a problem for me to have to learn to run a little slower to make sure you're safe.*

"I can still feel bad about it," Rin mumbled, his jaw pressed against Blue's neck muffling his words.

I don't feel bad about it, so you shouldn't either. Now, let's run and get this over with. I'm hungry.

Jim apparently agreed because he stood up from where he had been leaning against the nearby fence and clapped his hands. "One more time around and we'll call it done for the day."

Rin sat up straight in the saddle and let out a heavy breath of air. Blue was right, of course. It was ultimately Blue's decision how the race was going to be run, given he was the one doing the work. If he didn't mind having to work a bit harder, then all Rin could do was make it as easy for Blue as possible—and maybe reward him later when they were sharing the shower. He pushed that unhelpful thought from his mind and hurried to get his body into the right position. The sooner they finished this last run, the sooner they would be back at the house in the shower, and the sooner the rather decadent images filling Rin's head could become reality.

*

Blue wasn't just sleeping. He was practically unconscious, draped over Rin's body. He wasn't even gnawing at Rin's shoulder. In the years Rin had known Blue, he had never seen Blue sleep so deeply. Which didn't help the fact that Rin had to pee, and Blue was an unmovable blanket lying on top of his bladder.

It took some maneuvering, first carefully pulling his torso out from the grip of Blue's arms around him, and then shimmying his body to free his legs. Somehow, he managed it without waking Blue. Rin got both feet on the ground and wandered off toward the bathroom.

That day's training session had been particularly brutal for them both. It had been Rin's lone day off, so Jim had worked them the entire day with only a break for lunch. They hadn't even been able to go swimming, which had made Blue grumble, but they were starting to get it together. Rin could stay in position for long enough that Jim thought he could make it through an entire race, and Blue was able to run for a while without his glamor slipping once. They had to fake it long enough to win Mama the money, and they could just about do that now.

Jim had ended the very long day with a wide, conspiratorial grin at them. "I'll enter you in the next short race," he had told them after their last successful run around the pasture. "You're both ready to go. Take the rest of the evening to relax. I want to go have a quick shower before dinner." He'd nodded to them, unlocked the pasture gate, and found the path to head to the house. Mama was there waiting for him as was becoming their habit. The relationship she had with Jim was continuing to develop in ways that made Rin grind his teeth.

Rin firmly put that thought out of his mind as he fumbled around the bathroom, still half asleep. Jim's conversation from dinner a few hours ago was much more interesting to dwell on, anyway.

Jim had explained the fae heritage Rin inherited from his father was the reason he had recovered enough to walk without braces and crutches. Rin did vaguely remember a doctor or therapist remarking on how well his recovery was going back when he'd still had daily physical therapy sessions, but Mama had quickly deflected that line of thought. At the time, Rin had been in a sort of depressed fugue, so he didn't really remember any specifics.

"Have you tried recently?" Rin remembered Jim asking all those weeks ago when he still hadn't been sure his legs would allow him to stay on Blue's back long enough to win.

Rin hadn't. Blue did all the work when they went riding together. Rin had always let Blue's magic hold him in place and didn't have to do anything to keep them moving. It was an amazingly good shock when Rin realized Jim had been right.

Were Rin's legs magically healed back to the state they had been before the accident? Absolutely not. Yet, every day Jim had Rin up on Blue's back, working them both to total exhaustion, Rin felt his riding muscles returning. The muscle memory was there; he only had to regain the actual muscle. The real problem was the fact that his bones were far more brittle, and a fall from Blue's back could seriously injure him again, maybe too much even for his fae heritage to heal. They were being careful, though, and it was far too rewarding to stop now.

Rin finished up in the bathroom and returned to bed. He crawled under the covers next to Blue and was unsurprised when a moment later Blue rolled over to blanket him again. It was easy to fall right back to sleep and return to dreaming about the race to come.

*

There were heavy clouds low in the sky when Rin woke up again. Blue was still asleep, so Rin lay still and enjoyed the feeling of Blue's body pressed against his. There wasn't anything sexual about it; rather, it was about comfort and companionship. Rin valued moments like this one even more than the few times they had managed a more carnal morning.

It didn't matter to Mama.

"Get up or there won't be any breakfast!" she called through the door.

Rin sighed, and Blue let out a loud snort.

Can I eat her?

Rin laughed. "No, Blue, but I smell waffles. You can eat those."

Waffles? Blue lifted his head off Rin's shoulder and sniffed the air. *Yummy.*

He rolled off Rin with a happy whinny.

*

Too much running. I like to swim, not run. My legs hurt, my back hurts, and my glamor is tired. All I want to do is relax in my lake with my snack. I can't do that either, though, which is the saddest thing of all. Rin has work. I do go visit him, but he can't leave his post to spend time with me.

I used to be alone all the time in my lake. It

was how I preferred it, especially since when someone got too close, I knew they might eventually become prey. Rin changed that, brought me back to a family, so I would run for him even if I would much rather be swimming.

But there was so much running! Go, go, go all the time. Mama's horses like to run. Mary and Tildie run with me when I'm practicing, and they're happy. I am not happy about it. But the silly sisters couldn't swim, so maybe liking running wasn't strange to them.

The race has to be coming up soon. I want to be done with running so I can spend all day in my lake with my snack.

Sorry, Blue. You know this will help out Mama and I like riding when I'm working with you.

Most of the day you're not here! Running is only fun with you. I can pretend I'm stealing you away to suck out your bone marrow.

Creepy.

Or suck something else. That would be fun too!

*

Rin shut his diary with a snap, feeling his face flare with heat. Mama had better not ever read his diary. He wouldn't be able to look her in the eye again. Blue had zero shame. But at the same time, Rin wanted to pick up the pencil Blue had left next to the diary and write *Okay* underneath Blue's final comment.

To avoid temptation, he pushed his desk chair back and got to his feet. Blue was off practicing with Jim at the moment, which left Rin without much to do. Mama was at work, and he had finished all of his chores. Honestly, all Rin wanted to do was relax in Blue's lake with Blue. Usually on dark days, Rin could barely find the energy to move from his bed to the couch downstairs. The job was so draining that his lone day off was his only chance to recuperate, and normally it took him the full day to do so. This year, though, he felt much better.

Maybe the extra exercise he was getting working with Blue and Jim in the evenings had strengthened his body to the point that he couldn't enjoy just sitting around. He had hoped writing more in his diary would help, but Blue had kiboshed that idea. He honestly couldn't believe he was considering it, but as he wandered down the stairs, he started thinking about possible chores he could get done for Mama.

Jim had mentioned one of their sheds wasn't going to last the winter. It was easy enough to see which one. The roof was blackened on one side from rot, and the entire building was listing slightly. It was still structurally sound for the most part or Mama would have warned Rin away, but that wouldn't be true for much longer. Inside were their gardening tools, which they used in the spring to plant Blue's cucumbers. All of that would need a new home before the shed could be taken down.

There were rakes, hoes, and shovels hung on the walls. In the center of the shed was their wheelbarrow. Rin piled as much as he could into the wheelbarrow and carefully backed it out of the shed. He dumped its contents in the yard and went back for more.

Once the shed was empty, Rin paused to figure out where to relocate it all. The best place for it would probably be one of the empty stalls in the barn they weren't using. Once Blue won his race, Mama would be able to replace the shed entirely, and Rin would move everything back.

He had most of the stuff organized into neat piles when the sound of tires crunching on the drive made him look up. A pickup truck with a single-horse trailer on the back pulled to a stop in the yard, and a burly man hopped out of the cab. He was shorter than Rin, but his shoulders were doubly as wide. His beard was curly and unkempt and reached midway down his chest. It was also totally indistinguishable from his hair, which was as long and unbrushed.

"I've got a horse for you," the man grunted at Rin as he headed to the trailer.

"A horse?" Rin asked, unsure why the man was delivering anything to them.

"Yep. Ole Sheeba here had been wanting a crazy foal of her own, and Jim said Demon Blue was causing problems here. Sheeba'll set him straight nice and quick, let me tell you."

"Sheeba as in Queen of Sheeba, the horse that came in third in the Whitney last year?" Rin was gaping at the man, certain he was talking to a crazy person. The Whitney was a Grade I stakes race at Saratoga. It was second only to the Travers in races for the entire season. Placing in the Whitney was a big deal for a horse. Jim wouldn't waste a horse like Sheeba on a monster like Demon.

Yet the horse the man led out of the trailer was definitely Sheeba. Her distinctive dappled coat was impossible to miss, the shine of intelligence in her eyes told Rin she knew what she was about, and her sleek muscles said she could run.

"Where do you want her?" the man asked. Rin wordlessly pointed toward the empty paddock, still staring at Sheeba. Mama had had Grade I horses before, but not since the accident, and she certainly wouldn't have lent them out as easily as Jim was apparently willing to. Selling those Grade I horses had been the reason she was able to keep the farm for so long on a waitress's salary.

A pair of arms wrapped themselves around Rin's waist.

Why are you staring like that at another horsie? Do I have to get jealous?

"No, you don't have to get jealous, Blue," Rin replied with a laugh. "That's Sheeba."

"She'll take a bite out of Demon," Jim said, grinning as he passed them and went to greet the driver. Sheeba was nosing her way around the paddock, getting to know her new accommodations. Rin would have to fill her feed and water bins, but first he wanted to know what Jim was thinking.

"Sheeba and Demon. Are you crazy?" he asked Jim sharply.

Jim was unfazed. "I was thinking about sending Old Man Joe for Mary and Tildie, but I didn't want to presume anything. If your mother likes Sheeba, I'll look into sending Joe down too."

Rin had heard of Old Man Joe too. He had beaten one of Mama's horses in the Jim Dandy Grade II race two years before the accident and hadn't stopped there. He had long been retired, but he would be top-notch breeding stock for another ten years. Mama couldn't say no to a horse like that.

With the bloodlines she had fostered to get Mary and Tildie combined with Old Man Joe, Mama wouldn't only be looking at stakes races. She could actually think about the Travers. Heck, she could send a horse with breeding like that to the Triple Crown if she wanted. That was a horse breeder and trainer's dream. Rin was thinking about million-dollar horses in races with purses well above that. One win or one good sale of a foal, and they would never have to worry about money again.

Rin squeezed Blue's arms where they were still wrapped around him. There was no reason for Jim to be so generous unless he was serious about turning his business over to Mama for thirty years. The real question was whether Mama was going to finally capitulate.

The two men finished shaking hands, and the burly one, whose name Rin hadn't heard, got back in his truck. He turned around on the drive and headed off.

"He could have stayed for a few hours," Rin said tentatively. He was still shocked to see Sheeba's dappled coat prancing around their paddock.

"He doesn't like being away from his clan," Jim said with a shrug. "Wanted to get home before dinner."

He's a lower fairy, a dwarf, Blue explained. *Silly diggers*. All Rin knew about dwarfs was from animated movies with princesses, but the man did seem to fit the stereotype.

"Lower fairy?" Rin asked. So far, he knew about seelie versus unseelie, and that Blue was considered lesser because he was closer to animal than human.

"Means he's not as pretty or as powerful in magic as the fae. Dwarves are fairly insular anyway, but they're distant relations with the drow, so they're willing to work with me." Jim shrugged, but Rin had a strange feeling Jim was downplaying the importance of his connection.

Whatever. Want to go swimming?

Rin had to feed Sheeba, and he didn't know if Jim wanted them to practice his jockeying first, but Blue was practically vibrating against his back.

Jim just laughed, exactly like Mama would have in the same situation. "I'll make sure Sheeba gets settled. Go have fun."

Blue stepped away from Rin, and his body shimmered for a brief moment before his horse form appeared. Rin climbed on, able to hoist himself onto Blue's back without the aid of Blue's magic for the first time ever, and they headed off to Blue's lake.

*

Mama asked me if I was nervous. I tried laughing it off, but the honest answer is yes. Very much so.

I'm fine riding horses. I'm fine with Blue. Riding as a jockey in a race is a bit more than I am honestly ready for. Blue will be the one in charge. He'll be running as the horse in the race and making all the decisions like a jockey. I'm there because Blue can't run without a jockey on his back.

Will my legs hold out?

What if I fall? I'll get hurt, and we won't win the race, we won't get Mama's name back out there, and we won't win the money we need.

What if I hurt Blue? That would be completely unacceptable.

I have to keep reminding myself that all I need to do is hold on. Don't let my feet fall out of the stirrups, don't let my hands fall off the reins, and don't let my body fall off Blue's back. It's not nearly as much to focus on as what Blue has learned.

Jim signed Blue up for a Monday race. It's a nonclaiming maiden race for yearlings, which Blue is pretending to be. Everything we're doing is illegal. Both Mama and Jim could get banned from horse racing forever if they're caught faking a horse's papers.

The purse isn't particularly huge for the race in question, but Mama bet a good deal of what's left of her savings on the race. First place will only win a percentage; what's left will go to second, third, and fourth place. Mama could walk home with only a few hundred from Blue winning the race, but she should have closer to thirty thousand from betting on him. Her original five thousand dollars plus the fact that Blue's morning-line odds aren't looking spectacular will mean a big payout at the betting booths.

One glance at Blue's pedigree no doubt has bettors running in the opposite direction. Jim set it up so a completely unknown and untested horse is Blue's sire, and very few want to bet on something so uncertain. Blue chose Mary as his dam for the paperwork, but she never broke out of maiden despite her pedigree. Mama's name next to Blue's on the racing form will raise some eyebrows, but she's been out of the picture for so long people have no doubt forgotten about her strength as owner and trainer. The odds for Blue I last saw were seventy-six to one. Mama could win a lot of money off Blue if he wins.

When he wins.

I'm rambling. My poor diary is filling with lines of useless text. I apologize, Blue, that you have to read this (since I know you will eventually steal my diary again), but you're not here. Mama drove you to the track a few hours ago. You're spending the night in horse form in an uncomfortable stall. I might have a nice bed to sleep in, but without you here I don't honestly feel like sleeping.

I will see you tomorrow afternoon in the paddock before our race. Until then, I guess I'll try to sleep.

*

Rin had taken the day off work. It wasn't hard. He had gone into the officer's room where the captain in charge of roll call held court and informed them he would be out on Monday. The captain had written that down in his big book. Hopefully that message was then passed along to Freed, although chances were Rin's name would still be yelled at roll call and he would be marked absent until someone thought to actually check that captain's log.

One hand did not talk to the other at the Saratoga Race Course.

Even Rin's thoughts were rambling. He parked his car in the usual lot, climbed through the broken fence, and jaywalked across the street. The track was never busy on Mondays. This time he showed his jockey badge to the guard at the service gate, who didn't recognize Rin without the terrible uniform on and jumped to let him into the track with far more deference than Rin deserved.

The horses for the first race were walking down the horse path when Rin got to the crossing at Gate A. He waited patiently among the patrons and crossed when the path was clear again. He followed the horse path along the fence—the opposite side of the yard he usually patrolled—until he reached the jockey house. Jim was waiting for him when Rin stepped inside.

The red shirt Jim was wearing clashed terribly with the brown shade of skin his glamor gave him, but that was the uniform the valets wore, and Jim had designated himself as Rin's helper for this part of the race. Mama was with Blue.

"Let me find the sergeant here," Jim said after clapping Rin on the shoulder.

The woman he brought over a few seconds later was one of the sergeants who stood at roll call with Rin. The jockey escorts sector had the same roll call as Rin's sector, so he knew Sergeant Val's face even though he hadn't met her. She seemed like a nice enough lady, and there hadn't yet been any complaints or firings out of the jockey escorts this season—a record—so she must've known how to do her job correctly.

"This is a new jockey. He needs an escort to first aid," Jim explained.

Sergeant Val grunted, then turned to look at the milling crowd of guards. "Apple, do you have a jockey this race?"

"Nope," a girl replied with a grin. "You want me to run him over?"

"And bring him back," Sergeant Val added pointedly.

Apple nodded and waved her hand toward the rear of the jockey house. The building itself was old and split into two parts. The left half of the building was the men's changing room and the silks room in the back. The right half was administrative offices and a smaller changing room for the few female jockeys. The middle was open, and Apple led Rin through the divide and out a back gate Rin had never noticed before.

First aid was located on the first floor of the grandstand directly behind the carousel. Rin had directed patrons there before for Band-Aids and such but had never been there himself. He found it ironic he could walk from the parking lot to the jockey house on his own, but he had to be escorted from the jockey house to first aid. Definitely weird.

Apple held the door for him when they got to first aid and then settled into a chair by the door while Rin explained to the receptionist why he was there. He was led into a back room where a nurse walked in holding a sterile cup.

"We have your latest physical on file, and it looks good," she said as she passed him the cup and gestured to the nearby bathroom. Jim must have taken out any mention of the accident, or at the very least had forged a doctor's note saying he was okay to ride. All the track needed at the moment was a drug test.

Rin did his business and returned the filled cup to the nurse. She waved him toward the door, so he went back to Apple. They walked to the jockey house together where Jim took Rin in hand and led him into the men's locker room.

The uniform for a jockey consisted of an undershirt followed by a safety vest with his silks on top. Mama's silks were always blue-and-green stripes, but for Blue, they had gone with navy-blue-and-baby-blue stripes. Rin had compression shorts on his legs with the mandatory white pants over them. On his feet went the most uncomfortable black riding boots he had ever worn. They went nearly to his knees and looked like cheap plastic, but they were extremely expensive.

The majority of the jockeys were from Mexico and South and Central American countries, and they chatted in Spanish with the occasional bit of English thrown in. All Rin could really stay focused on was how he had to remember to bend his knees in order to stay on Blue's back.

Jim stepped away to study Rin in his uniform and nodded like he was pleased with what he saw.

"You look the part. You'll get a few more pounds because you're an apprentice jockey, so we don't have to worry about weight either. Let me get the saddle together, and we'll be good to go."

Jim stepped away for a moment to putter around the cubby Rin had been given for the day. The door opened and the jockeys from the last race came inside. Most of them were covered head-to-toe in the muck from the dirt track, but since Rin and Blue were running in the grass, they didn't have to worry about that. The jockeys hurried to pull their dirty clothes off and wash off in the showers. Their valets set out fresh pants and silks for them.

"Haven't seen you before," the man using the cubby next to Rin's remarked.

"I'm new," Rin explained.

The jockey grinned at him. "Welcome. It's a wild ride, but I love it."

"That's why I'm here," Rin replied with a shrug, hoping his words sounded sincere.

The overhead speakers crackled to life, and the voice of the clerk of scales sounded through the room. "All out, check, check, all out."

Rin waved goodbye to the friendly jockey and joined the group of dressed jockeys heading outside. The scale was in the open area between the locker room and the administrative office. Jim was waiting for Rin there. He thrust a saddle and straps into Rin's hands, and Rin got onto the scale when it was his turn.

The heaviest part of the saddle was the irons, or the stirrups, but for Blue, they were made of pure silver so they didn't burn him. They jangled against Rin's side as he climbed onto the scale. It read one-twenty-six, which was Rin's weight without the heavy saddle he was holding. Jim winked when Rin glanced at him to see if it was right.

"Three," Jim called. The clerk input the number and Rin's weight into the computer. Jim took the saddle from Rin and handed over a whip as Rin climbed down so another jockey could take his place on the scale. Jim helped Rin pin the number three to Rin's sleeve. "Come out to the paddock with the rest of the jockeys," he instructed.

Jim took the saddle to a nearby table to get it situated with the foam pad and the blue saddle blanket with a white number three emblazoned on it, then headed out of the jockey room.

Rin swallowed hard and leaned against a nearby table with pretended nonchalance. His stomach was in knots, roiling and rumbling unhappily. All he needed to do was stay on Blue's back. Blue would be doing all the hard work and decision-making, yet Rin couldn't help being nervous.

There was so much riding on this one race. Mama's money and reputation, Jim's hopes for his horses, and even Rin's confidence in himself. He had been injured, useless for anything important, for so long. He hadn't felt as strong as he did at this moment in ages, and one mistake could end all that in seconds.

"All out for the fifth race! All out!" the clerk of scales called into the loudspeaker. Rin took a deep breath to steady himself while the jockeys filed out of the locker room. Some were crossing themselves while others snapped their whips to warm up. Rin followed them as they walked out of the jockey area and into the crowd of patrons. A uniformed security guard was walking with Rin as they all headed to the nearby horse path. Rin had never worked as a jockey escort before, but they were a tight-knit bunch. They usually hung out together before and after their shifts, unknowingly excluding other guards like Rin who would have enjoyed a night out with people his age.

Rin pushed those thoughts from his mind. The dirt under his feet was familiar. He had walked in this same path with his mother all those years ago, and even now as a guard he occasionally got to take the path to get somewhere. He had even been in the paddock recently for the Diana Grade I race. That didn't stop his nerves from making his hands shake. He gripped his whip tighter and walked into the paddock itself.

He caught sight of Blue immediately and headed over to him. Each horse had a designated area to walk around in; Blue was standing next to a tree with a number three nailed to it. He looked amazingly normal. His current shade of blue was perfect, and there was no sign of fangs or horns. His hooves appeared to be shod, although Rin knew that was an illusion too. The saddle was on Blue's back, and Mama was loosely holding the lead attached to Blue's halter.

Rin threw his arms around Blue's neck and held tight for a brief moment.

This is gonna be fun, Blue insisted. *We're gonna run superfast and make all the other horsies eat our dust.*

"You're going to keep to the speed the race demands, Blue," Jim admonished sharply. "No faster than a regular horse can run."

Yeah, yeah. Blue let out a heavy snort of air through his nose. *I'll remember.*

"Even with your magic to hold Rin in place, make sure not to jostle him too much. Rin has made amazing progress, but he's not at full strength yet."

"They'll both do fine," Mama cut in. "Blue knows how to run, and Rin knows how to ride. I have no worries." She sounded sincere. As if to punctuate Mama's words, the one horse let out an aggressive squeal as he was led past Blue toward his own marked tree.

That one doesn't like me, Blue grumbled.

"He knows you're going to beat him," Rin replied, picking up on Mama and Jim's jovial moods and running with it. He was with Blue, so nothing could go wrong. Nerves had no place here.

"Line them up, please," one of the men in charge of the paddock called. They obeyed, leaving the circle around the tree and joining the rest of the horses in the show ring that encircled the paddock and led out to the track. They were all lined up by the number on their saddle blanket. Rin, Mama, and Jim walked alongside Blue as he followed the two horse. All the horses stopped for a long moment, and their hot-walkers had them circle.

The same man was at the head of the horses. "Riders up!" he yelled.

"Ready?" Mama said softly.

Rin nodded. He reached up to grip the long reins high on Blue's back and jumped upward with one foot held back in the air. Mama caught his foot and used her leverage to toss him up and onto Blue's back. Rin landed neatly in the saddle, and the familiar shiver of Blue's magic ran through him.

Blue walked behind the two horse as Rin carefully fit his feet into the irons. He checked his balance and got situated in the saddle before picking up the reins to knot them to the correct length.

Do I have to lift my tail too? Blue asked grumpily. *Since I'm pretending to be a real horse?*

Rin looked up just in time to see the two horse lift his tail to poo.

"Please keep your tail right where it is, Blue," Rin insisted. Mama let out a snort of laughter at their side.

The track came into view quickly. An outrider was waiting for them as Mama unhooked her lead, but Mama hurriedly waved him off. Blue could warm up on his own. The bugle started playing its signature *dun dun dum dundundum dundundum dum dum dum duuummm.*

Blue trotted onto the dirt track; his skin and magic shivered in disgust underneath Rin's legs.

This is gross, Blue whined. The dirt track looked like regular brown dirt, but after one hundred and fifty years of horses lifting their tails on it, Rin knew Blue was right. It was pretty gross.

"That's why we're running on the grass turf," Rin reminded him. "Let's get warmed up."

Blue whinnied in agreement and picked up his pace. He purposefully jumped around and spun in a tight circle to ensure that between his magic and Rin's tenuous grip, Rin would stay on his back. They arrived at the starting gate ahead of the rest of the horses and crossed over onto the turf track to wait.

There were a dozen people in red shirts and black safety vests waiting by the gate. One of them approached Rin and Blue.

"Blue can get in the gate without help," Rin explained when the man reached for Blue's bridle. Blue allowed Rin to ride him and had tolerated the necessity of Mama holding him, but he wouldn't allow a total stranger to do that. The man looked skeptical but stepped away to grab another horse as the rest got to them.

The one horse squealed aggressively as he was led past Blue and into the gate. The two joined him, and then Blue stepped forward to follow. The starting gate was a long contraption that had to be pulled around the track by a tractor. It was the same odd shade of green as the jockey room, and each individual gate was barely large enough to hold a horse and rider. Blue shivered unhappily at the close quarters.

Hurry up, he grumbled. *I wanna run already!*

It didn't take too long for all seven horses to be loaded. There was a moment of silence as anticipation grew. Rin took in a deep breath and let it out slowly. He was shaking slightly and his stomach was sour with nerves, but his hands were still firm on the reins. He could do this—they could do this.

With a shout and a loud bell ringing overhead, the gates popped open. All the horses surged forward, urged by their riders, and Blue leaped to the front.

The snorting and panting of horses, the jockeys urging them on, and the powerful *thump-thump-thump-thump* as hooves pounded into the grass sounded around Rin, almost in time to the heavy beat of his pounding heart. Blue didn't speak; he was focused on running and staying in front of the herd while not going too fast. Rin held on, his knees flexing in time with Blue and his hands tight around the reins.

He could see the fence line to their right and the grass below them vanishing beneath Blue's hooves as they flew along the track. Behind him, more horses snorted, their heavy breaths sounding along with the beat of their gallop. The fence line curved sharply as they rounded the turn and headed into the top of the stretch. Rin's thighs were burning, and Blue's sides were heaving beneath him, but the butterflies and the shaking were both gone. Rin was flying, and if he had the breath for it, he felt like laughter would be bubbling up. This was so much better than running in circles around the paddock, and he couldn't stop the wide grin on his face.

They reached the edge of the grandstand still in the lead. The wall of sound as hundreds—if not thousands—of patrons all cheered and screamed for their favorite to go just a bit faster hit Rin and reverberated around them as they headed toward the finish line.

And, suddenly, it was over.

Rin hadn't heard it over the horses, but he knew from experience what must have gone through the overhead speakers in the grandstand and clubhouse:

"And they're off! Kelpie Blue jumps in front with Destiny's Dream right behind. Overunder is strong in third. Lolly Pop Kid is next in line with Hoppy Kitten, Geeserunner, and Longshot Attempt in the rear as they come up the backstretch. And Kelpie Blue continues to lead the pack. Overunder has moved up to second as Destiny's Dream is running out of steam. They've reached the top of the stretch, and here comes Longshot Attempt! Longshot Attempt is surging on the outside. He's passed Geeserunner and Hoppy Kitten, but no one can catch up to Kelpie Blue! It's Kelpie Blue as they come to the line!

It's Kelpie Blue taking the race wire to wire! Followed by Overunder, Longshot Attempt, and Lolly Pop Kid in fourth."

The race had only taken a little over a minute to run. Rin let his butt settle into the saddle as Blue began to slow. His legs ached, and his hands were clenched tightly around the reins. Magic tingled up through the saddle under his butt, pinning him in place on Blue's back, so Rin finally let his body relax, but his head was still flying.

That was...it was...wow! "We did it!" Rin crowed.

I was fastest, Blue agreed excitedly. He didn't even sound out of breath.

"Yes, you were!" They had done it. Rin had stayed on Blue's back, and they had won the race. He could barely believe it, but now Mama would be able to start rebuilding both her farm and her reputation.

They turned to head back to the finish line. The one horse danced sideways as Blue went by, but they both ignored him. Mama and Jim were waiting in front of the winner's circle. Blue hurried to meet up with them.

Ta da! Blue struck a pose and let out a happy whinny.

"Congratulations!" Mama crowed. She was holding a small bucket filled with ice water. She dipped a sponge into the water before handing it up to Rin. Blue let out a happy shiver as Rin doused his neck.

Mama took the sponge and then waved for Blue to head into the winner's circle.

The winner's circle was supposed to be one of the nicest areas at the track. The fence around it was iron painted black, and the flower boxes hanging from it overflowed with blooms. The floor was fake brick tile that could easily be hosed down if a horse made a mess while standing on it.

Blue pranced inside. He stood still while Mama and Jim stood next to them and a picture was taken.

"In the winner's circle we have Kelpie Blue, owned and trained by Lizzy Roark Stables, and ridden by Rin Roark," the announcer called overhead.

"I need to get weighed again," Rin explained to Blue once the announcer finished. The magic holding Rin in place dissipated as Blue let out a sigh.

We'll run more at home, Blue said.

Rin swung one leg over Blue's side and slid to the ground. He unhooked the saddle with Jim's help and carried it across the winner's circle to the scale.

"You have to go back to the barn for now, Blue," Mama called. Blue sighed heavily from over Rin's shoulder but obediently turned to follow Mama out of the winner's circle.

The last of the racehorses were being led past the winner's circle toward the top of the stretch, where they could leave the track. They were all still blowing heavily through their noses, snorting loudly as their nostrils vibrated with every breath. Blue was barely winded, but Rin's thighs were burning. He had managed to stay in the proper jockey's riding stance the entire time, and as his adrenaline faded, he was starting to feel it.

Rin was stepping off the scale, the saddle held out for Jim to take from him, when Blue yelled.

The one horse was just dropping his rear hooves back to the ground with his handlers yanking him away, and Blue was rolling back to his feet when Rin looked over.

"Blue!" Rin yelled. He dropped the saddle, missing Jim's arms entirely, and hurried over to Blue's side.

His hide was rippling, the natural blued shade fading to look more like its normal shade of navy.

"Keep it together, Blue," Jim said soothingly from behind Rin.

But it hurts! Blue whined. He was only standing on three legs, holding his left foreleg in the air.

Rin reached his side at the same time as Jim and gently stroked Blue's neck. Jim wrapped one arm under Blue's chest as if he could hold Blue's weight.

"We've got to walk off the track," Jim hissed under his breath as two people Rin knew were veterinarians approached. "If you get put in the horse ambulance, they won't let you go without a full exam." And Blue was barely holding on to his glamor at the moment.

"Come on, Blue, we only need to get off the track," Rin added encouragingly.

"I'll get the trailer," Mama called. "Meet you there." She ran off with Rin's saddle in hand. Blue took one halting step and then another as Rin kept petting Blue's neck. It was all he could do. Blue needed to walk off on his own to keep the vets from taking charge. Every step with his injured leg caused another pained shiver to run through him, but with Jim's support, he was doing it.

"Come on, Blue. You can do it." Rin murmured under his breath over and over. The winner's circle was far from the horse path at the top of the stretch where Mama could meet them. Blue limped the length of the grandstand slowly, but he did it.

Mama's familiar car with the horse trailer hooked to the back was waiting for them at the gate. Mama was arguing with a vet who also had the horse ambulance pulled up.

"I'm bringing him to my own vet," Mama said. "The NYRA vets euthanize first, X-ray second, and I won't be letting you anywhere near this horse."

The rear doors of the horse trailer were open, and Jim helped Blue inside. Rin climbed in with him as Blue sank to the ground, and Jim shut the door behind them. The truck started up a moment later, so Mama must have won her argument.

It took a few moments for Mama to navigate the horse path, but once they had turned onto Union Avenue, Rin finally relaxed.

"Okay, Blue. You can let go now."

With a sob, Blue let his glamor go. Rin expected to see his water horse body appear, but instead Blue took his human shape. His skin was still blue, and his ears pointed. There were horns on his head and his hair was thick and navy blue. Blue wrapped his good arm around Rin's waist and buried his face in Rin's silks.

Ow. Owwie. Ow. Blue sobbed.

"What can I do to help?" Rin asked, trying not to sound frantic. How did he help Blue get better? In all their years of living together, it had always been Rin who was injured; this turnaround was not fun in the least.

Blue didn't answer, just continued crying. Rin held him tightly, careful of the arm, and desperately wished there was something he could do. Rin wanted to take the pain away or help set the broken bone. He wanted Blue to get better, to not have a broken arm at all.

The drive didn't take too long. Soon enough, the tires went over the familiar bumps as they transferred from smooth pavement to the packed dirt of the driveway. Mama stopped the car in front of the house, and a few moments later she and Jim were pulling open the trailer doors to let Blue and Rin out.

Blue slowly unwound his body from Rin's and staggered to his feet. His arm was still tucked protectively against his chest, but his cheeks were beginning to dry. Rin hurried to stand up as well so he could support Blue if Blue needed him. They both climbed out of the back of the trailer and stood blinking in the afternoon sunlight.

"Let me see, Blue," Jim said gently. He held out one hand toward Blue but waited for Blue to haltingly uncurl his injured arm and hold it out for Jim to see.

Jim very carefully ran his fingers down Blue's arm, prodding where Blue had gotten kicked. Every hiss and whimper of pain made Rin flinch, but Blue was being remarkably stoic about it.

"I could have sworn your arm was completely broken, Blue," Jim said. He sounded contemplative and slightly concerned. "I was trying to figure out a way to convince you to come Underhill with me to go see a healer, but right now, I'm only sensing the remnants of a hairline fracture."

My snack told me to get better, Blue explained proudly.

"Did he?" Jim replied. He turned toward Rin, looking even more curious. "Lizzy, do you happen to know what type of fae Rin's father was?"

Mama sighed. "No. He looked human enough at the time, but Blue can make himself look completely human when he wants, so who knows what he really looked like. I was with him three months before he was called away. I waited another four months for him to come back until I couldn't hide the pregnancy any longer and had to leave."

"Could be one of Dian's brood," Jim murmured, looking sharply at Rin. "Do you remember what he looked like?"

Mama laughed. "I do, but he's hard to describe. I think that was part of his glamor, actually, that I wouldn't entirely remember. But I know Rin has his eyes."

"Blue eyes do run in Dian Cecht's line," Jim replied.

"Who's Dian Cecht?" Rin asked, mangling the Celtic but wanting to know more about his father.

"Dian Cecht and his offspring are some of the greatest healers the seelie sidhe have ever known. Dian returned Nuada's lost arm to him, and then Miach, Dian's son, perfected the arm so Nuada might return to the throne. There's no telling which of his line fathered you, Rin, but you did somehow manage to heal Blue."

My snack is amazing, Blue added firmly. *He made the pain go away.*

"Well, mostly," Jim agreed with a glance at how stiffly Blue was still holding his arm. "You won't be changing into your horse form for a while. Too much weight on that foreleg could refracture it."

No more riding? Blue asked, sounding disappointed. *What about swimming?*

Jim laughed, but Rin knew how serious a question that was. Not being able to swim would be catastrophic for Blue. Anyone who knew Blue knew that, and Jim wasn't any different.

"As long as you're careful, you can swim." Jim patted Blue on the shoulder one last time before turning his focus back to Rin. "And it seems like I need to go

Underhill to ask Dian Cecht some uncomfortable questions."

"Are you staying for dinner?" Mama asked. She brushed her hair out of her face, and Rin realized how disheveled she looked. She must have sprinted to get the car to the horse path in time and then had sat in the front of the car with no idea how injured Blue was in the back. She had lived through one child severely injured once, and the idea that Blue might be hurt too must have hurt her.

Jim must have seen what Rin was seeing. He smiled slightly and nodded. "I'll stay for dinner and head back Underhill afterward. And I'll call someone to pick up our cars and such from the track."

Rin had no doubt Jim was a good guy. Even if Rin didn't know everything about Jim, including most of his past, there was no denying that fact. He was good for Mama, and Rin could finally put aside his jealousy and let Mama smile back at Jim without interruption.

"Come on, Blue. We should get ice on your arm before it swells," Rin said. He wrapped an arm over Blue's shoulder, glad when Blue pressed close with a soft whinny, and headed inside the house.

*

Blue is still in pain, and I feel so bad for him! I don't know what to do to make him better except keep thinking healing thoughts. That's what worked in the horse trailer, so right now I'm lying in bed with him, thinking desperate thoughts about bones knitting together. Blue keeps whimpering slightly in his sleep, so I know it's not working anymore.

Maybe there's a limit to what my healing power can do?

I have no idea if what Jim said about my father is true. I didn't have time to look up Dian Cecht (Did I spell that right? I think I did...) on the computer. Sure, I've always wondered about my father, and lately I've been suspecting he's someone like Blue, but I never thought he might be a full sidhe. Not once. And the idea that I can do magic is crazy, but Blue insists I healed his arm.

It's a lot to take in, to be honest. It's easier to write those worries into this diary for Blue to read later rather than say anything out loud. It's also easier to keep thinking thoughts about Blue getting better rather than about what mysterious powers I might have.

Mama might be a cowboy, but I certainly am not.

I always thought I was a cowboy. Even when my body was broken and I couldn't leave my bed for months, I still thought of myself as one. It's not fun at all to suddenly learn that maybe I'm part fish, like Blue.

I am not a fishy!

*

Rin saw what Blue had written in the margin next to his latest diary entry and let out a snort of laughter. He turned toward Blue, who was still curled under the covers in bed, wondering when in the middle of the night Blue had gotten up to read and annotate his diary.

"You're not a fish," Rin finally said.

Blue slowly pulled the covers away from his face with his good arm. He was pouting at Rin.

Not a fishy, he insisted.

"You're a horse," Rin insisted back. "Just one that can breathe underwater like a fish."

Blue growled playfully at Rin. *I am not like a fish.*

"You have a strong tail like a fish and webbed fins like a fish," Rin continued teasingly, holding back laughter only by biting his lip.

Blue growled again and lunged for Rin. They fell onto the floor in a tangle of limbs, Blue's broken arm still carefully pressed to his chest where it wouldn't get bumped. Blue ended up sitting on Rin's stomach. He leaned over Rin so their faces were inches apart.

Not. A. Fish.

Rin couldn't stop the laughter that escaped him. Blue let out a whinnying chuckle of his own and then fused their lips together.

Magic tingled between them, the familiar pull of Blue's sticky magic keeping their lips tight, and Rin arched into it gladly. Blue shifted around until he was lying on top of Rin, and their lips separated with a spark of power that did evil things to Rin's body. He was hard and could feel Blue's length pressing against his thigh.

Blue licked up Rin's neck and nibbled along his chin, and all Rin could do was gasp and thrust his hips upward to rub his body against Blue, who obligingly pressed down to provide the desperately needed friction.

So delicious, my pretty snack, Blue murmured. He took Rin's ear between his teeth and bit down lightly before licking over the aching spot with his tongue. Rin groaned. His hands ended up on Blue's back at some point, and he obligingly dragged his nails down Blue's spine. Blue whinnied, and his hips jerked against Rin's.

Rin was so close, and each time their hips pressed together, he let out a little gasp. Blue ground their hips together harder and pressed his face into the crease between Rin's neck and shoulder. There was a brief flash of pain as Blue bit deep, but his hips rubbed against Rin in exactly the right way, and Rin came, hard. His hips jerked involuntarily against Blue's body, and Blue abruptly pulled his teeth out of Rin's shoulder and arched his spine backward to press his groin tighter against Rin as he came too.

It took a while for clarity to return to Rin's frazzled brain, but when he dropped back down to earth, he found Blue still lying on him, contentedly licking at the blood seeping from Rin's neck.

"You bit me?" Rin asked. His voice wasn't quite right, still low with remembered pleasure and his words half sighed instead of spoken.

Blue rumbled happily. *You are the best, most delicious snack ever.* He licked more blood off Rin's neck and then pulled back enough that Rin could see his face. *It means you're mine, and no one else can steal you for their snack.*

Blue bent down for a kiss, copper-flavored and slightly tangy in a way Rin had never tasted before. It wasn't a bad taste, at all. In fact, Rin wouldn't mind tasting more of his own blood on Blue's lips.

"I should bite you next time," Rin murmured against Blue's lips before arching his neck upward to press them firmly together.

Blue purred, but before he could answer, Mama's voice rang up the stairs.

"Breakfast in five, boys. Get down here or don't get fed."

"So much for cuddling," Rin sighed, but he still tilted his head to the side so Blue could lick the last of the blood away before taking one last, lingering, and blood-soaked kiss.

Blue peeled himself off Rin, their damp pajama pants stuck together where the come had started to dry.

"Ugh, let's get cleaned up really quickly," Rin grumbled even as Blue whined lowly. "We'll feed ourselves, feed the horses, and see if Mama will let us escape to the lake."

We can't ride, Blue grumbled with an unhappy glance down where Jim had tightly wrapped his forearm before heading to Underhill last night.

"So we'll walk. And we'll swim. It'll be fun." Rin grinned at Blue and went to go find clean pants and a high-necked shirt to cover the bite mark on his neck.

I like fun, Blue replied, his voice low and rumbling. Rin licked his lips as his body tightened in anticipation. They hadn't had sex in Blue's lake yet, but maybe that would change this afternoon. Rin couldn't wait.

Chapter Five

The day had started perfectly fine. A mutual round of pleasure before breakfast followed by delicious pancakes drizzled in syrup. They had then gone outside to feed and water the horses and found Demon sulking in one corner of Sheeba's corral. Sheeba looked unbelievably smug, and Blue commented she had gotten what she wanted from Demon, a foal, and had put the bastard horse in his place afterward.

Only once they finished laughing had Blue let Demon out of Sheeba's corral. Demon had never been so cooperative in his life, eager to get as far away from Sheeba as he could. Hopefully, he had learned his lesson and would stop savaging the mares. Mama wanted to get a foal out of Mary or Tildie from him, but she hadn't dared chance it before now.

After their chores were completed, Rin and Blue had headed off to the lake. It was a dark day at the track, so Rin didn't have to worry about work. Today was all about play and pleasure, and pleasure had definitely been had.

Now, though, Rin wished he had stayed at the house for just a little longer. Mama had taken the day off at the restaurant so she could start making the phone calls and such that needed to be done to get her breeding and training business going again. Jim's representative was going to the track tomorrow to pick up all their winnings.

Rin smelled it before they walked high enough up the hill on their way back from the lake to be able to see what his nose was telling him.

Fire.

The smoke was acrid smelling in the breeze and dark gray as it billowed upward from the house and barns ahead.

"Mama!" Rin yelled. He sprinted toward the house. Blue flashed past him, faster even when confined to a human form.

Rin coughed as the wind blew smoke across his face and tried to hurry even more, hoping he wouldn't slip in one of the hoof scars on the path. This wasn't an ordinary fire, not if the house and the barns were on fire, which he could see they were. A fire at the house couldn't jump the distance across the driveway and paddocks to reach the barn. Someone had to have set it, which meant they had needed to get Mama out of the way first.

She would have stopped them had she been able.

"Mama!" Rin yelled as he rushed into the yard. "Mama!"

I can't find her! Blue yelled. Blue ran out of the house and into the burning barn, but Rin didn't dare follow. Blue could hold his breath for long enough to avoid the smoke, but Rin would only be a liability.

A shape slowly became visible in the smoke covering the driveway. A man was walking toward Rin, but Rin didn't recognize him.

"Blue," Rin called, hoping Blue would be able to reason with the stranger, or at least intimidate him into leaving.

"I followed them for a mile, but they got to the woods and a door to Underhill before I could catch them," Jim said. Rin blinked and squinted. The man walking toward him didn't look anything like Jim, but the words were in Jim's voice, and they had definitely come out of the stranger's mouth. Although, both Jim and the stranger shared the same very black skin.

The man had two ram's horns coming out of the sides of his head and curling behind his ears. His ears were pointed and long, longer even than Blue's. It was the eyes, though, that finally convinced Rin he was looking at Jim. They looked exactly the same even if Jim's face suddenly had severely pointed cheekbones and chin.

Jim turned toward the house and spat something. He waved his hand, and the fire went out. He did the same for the big barn.

"Where's Mama?" Rin asked desperately. Blue appeared and hurried to Rin's side with a querying neigh of his own.

Jim growled, and Rin involuntarily pressed his body against Blue's in response. Jim had always been so nice; even when they had first met and he had tried to curse Rin, he hadn't been this scary.

"They grabbed her," Jim snarled, "and set the place on fire to distract me while they ran. Me, one of the best trackers the seelie sidhe can boast, be distracted by some fire? Hah. But they got the jump on me." He sounded absolutely furious. He spat some incomprehensible words again, and the last of the fire went out with a final puff of smoke.

"Where's Mama?" Rin repeated, dread growing in his stomach.

"They took her Underhill!" Jim yelled. He stomped forward, fully out of the wispy, dissipating smoke, but his eyes were still spitting fire.

Why would someone take Mama to Underhill? Blue asked. He sounded calm, but his voice had the slightest waver that said he most definitely wasn't calm at all.

"I don't know," Jim said, and now he sounded defeated instead of furious. "Lizzy is human. Even her having a child of the sidhe isn't unusual enough for someone to pull her Underhill. There must have been another reason."

Rin didn't have an answer, just fear and worry churning in his gut and making his hands shake. No one else apparently had an answer either because they were all silent until the crunch of tires on the drive had everyone jumping in surprise.

Jim's horns vanished, replaced by his more familiar, human form. Blue also became much less blue. Rin recognized the car as it parked right in front of them and had to grit his teeth as James Wesley climbed out.

"It looks like you've been having some problems," Wesley said smarmily. His bleached head turned to look at the burnt porch of the house and the roof of the large barn. "Have you reconsidered my offer? I could take this entire dump off your hands."

It hadn't been an offer the last time Wesley had shown up here. Unless the threat of a lawsuit could somehow be considered genial, which Rin doubted. Wesley smiled, and the façade of geniality vanished.

Shark, Blue whispered.

"And where is dear Lizzy? At a time like this, when her business is on fire, she's nowhere to be found? How irresponsible."

"What do you want, Wesley?" Jim growled through his teeth.

"With Lizzy gone, you don't have anyone to train your horses," Wesley continued. He was acting completely cool, as if Jim's growls and the last of the smoke blowing through the yard didn't faze him. "Your foolish merger will go under, and you'll lose everything. Let me help you out. I can see Sheeba there, and I know Lizzy keeps two other mares. I have also heard that you're readying Old

Man Joe for transport. If all four horses are shipped to my stables, I'll bet dear Lizzy will come stumbling back home. Unharmed. You have three days."

Wesley grinned at them again, not bothering to hide the sheer glee from his eyes. A shiver went down Rin's spine, and Jim let out another growl. Wesley climbed into his car and reversed it down the drive.

I thought you said Mama was taken Underhill. That evil shark said he has her! Blue let out a whinny as he spoke.

"He must have some sort of unseelie connections," Jim snarled. He hadn't moved, still staring at the road where the car had driven out of sight, but his hands were shaking with rage. Suddenly, he spun and froze Rin and Blue in place with the fury in his eyes. "We need to get her back before Wesley tries anything else."

"What do we do?" Rin asked in complete agreement. He was scared for Mama and would do just about anything to get her back.

"You and Blue need to go Underhill," Jim said after a moment of thought. "I can track her there, but my mixed heritage will bar me from places you and Blue will have no problem going. Together, you'll have a better chance of success. I'm going to stay here. If I can figure out what Wesley is paying the unseelie with, I might be able to shut him down and get Lizzy out from this side of the hill."

Rin nodded. He would do anything to get Mama back even if it meant going to the mysterious land of the fae.

"Good. Go pack a backpack. Blue, you know what sorts of things you should bring. Don't forget to give Rin a rundown of the dos and don'ts of Underhill." Jim pulled his cell phone out of his pocket as he finished speaking and punched in a number.

Come on, Blue said insistently. He headed into the house, and Rin followed.

It smelled smoky inside, but Rin couldn't see any sign of damage as he walked through the house and up the stairs. Mama would probably have to put on a new roof, but as long as it didn't rain before then, they wouldn't need to replace anything else. Blue had already unearthed Rin's old school backpack from the closet by the time Rin caught up and was rummaging through Rin's drawers. He stuffed a pair of jeans, boxers, and a shirt into the bag from Rin's clothes, then repeated it with a set of his own. Rin saw his diary go into the backpack too.

Let's get some food, Blue said. He trotted out of the bedroom, but he was waiting at the top of the stairs for Rin to catch up. *You have to be really, really careful in Underhill. People are mean, and everyone has an agenda. Try not to talk to anyone without me there because they'll try to trick you into agreeing to do something or give something to them you won't want to.*

"Okay," Rin replied seriously. He was going to be traveling in a completely new world, one of magic, where creatures like Blue, Jim, and Rin's father came from. He had to be prepared for weird things, even weirder than everything he had learned about Blue so far.

Don't say thank you for anything because they'll think you owe them a favor, and when Underhill collects, they'll collect in blood. Don't eat any food you see, especially if someone gives it to you, but if you see it hanging from a tree, it's probably still deadly.

"Is there anything good about Underhill?" Rin asked. He led the way into the kitchen and into the pantry where they kept food that would last a few days, which he stuffed in the backpack. He also grabbed a few water bottles to fill at the tap since, if the food was deadly, there was no telling whether the water would be drinkable.

It's very beautiful, Blue replied. He held the bag open for everything Rin had found. *Come on, we need to find a mushroom circle in the forest before it gets dark.*

"Huh?" Rin helped Blue zip the bag, and they headed outside.

Mushroom circles are a doorway to Underhill. Step into one with the intent to travel there, and they'll bring us inside.

"Okay. Let's do this."

The road to the forest was a familiar one since Blue's lake was on the way. They stepped onto the pockmarked path, and Rin set his chin as firmly as he set his feet on the ground. They would find Mama, survive Underhill, and save the business from Wesley.

They had to.

*

My mama had told me how she was going to get to Underhill when she went to save our lake. When I followed her, I found a mushroom circle and managed to get to Underhill on my own. My family's lake was nice; it was so perfectly comfortable. The sand on the bottom was soft and excellent for burrowing into for an afternoon nap, and the water was clear blue and always warmed by the sun.

Underhill was even bluer and clearer if that makes any sense.

Rin and I stepped out of our mushroom circle, and my snack stopped and stared for ten minutes straight, trying to see everything because everything was so worth seeing. He handled it so much better than I did my first time.

Somehow, the color blue was so much bluer. It almost had an inner glow, like it was backlit with something that intensified the various shades and hues that made blue blue. I swear, my pretty little snack, who I know will end up reading this at some point, I stared at my arm for the first five minutes, then at the sky overhead for the next ten.

I finally pulled away from all the pretty and started walking. My mother was here somewhere, and maybe the sidhe she had found to help us was here too. I walked and walked and walked. The spell that was Underhill had me good and trapped. If you just walk with no end goal in mind, the road is endless. It's like with the mushroom circles. You could stand in one all day, but without the will to direct the door to open, you won't go anywhere.

I eventually found a lake. The sun hadn't set—it hadn't moved an inch in the sky—but all four of my legs were aching, and my poor hooves desperately wanted some cool water to rest in. I jumped into the lake, screamed, and jumped right out.

It was salt water. A saltwater lake. Salt wasn't good for my skin and scales, and my skin was burning. It didn't help I was still a bit green from living in my parents' tainted lake.

Now I had a goal. I had to find somewhere safe where I could wash off the icky salt and to find somewhere to rest that wouldn't hurt me more. I focused on my goal, and as I limped along, the scenery began to slowly change around me until a small mansion appeared ahead. I somehow made it to the front door, and I know I knocked, but the rest of that day was a complete blank.

Jim says I passed out. Well, I was a small

kelpie back then, so maybe I did pass out. I don't faint now that I'm all big and grown. Don't worry, my pretty little snackable. I figured out the salt-water thing, so I won't get hurt again. Jim taught me that. He taught me a lot of things: about Underhill, my abilities as a kelpie, and life in general.

I stayed with him for a very long time. Learning first, then searching for my mama—which Jim had been doing all along—but Underhill is still a scary place. I am a creature of Underhill as all magical creatures are, but I had been born and bred in the human world. No matter how much time I spent in Underhill, I couldn't settle.

Jim found me my new lake a few steps outside of Underhill where I lived for a long time until my silly snack collapsed on my beach.

You know the rest of the story from there, Rin.

I do, Blue. Thank you for sharing this with me.

It's hard to say some stuff aloud. I get why you wanted to put the things in your head onto a page. It's easier to share it that way.

This was supposed to be a <u>private</u> diary, Blue!

Now you're just being silly.

*

Rin was smiling as he closed his diary yet again. Blue had left the diary right on top of the bag when he had handed it to Rin so Rin could get some food. The words inside were personal to Blue.

There was plenty Rin knew about Blue. The story of why Blue had left his lake somewhere in Europe and how he had come to the lake at home was one Rin had heard dozens of times, but the nuances of Blue's feelings always had a different level of depth every time.

Plus, the flirting they did after the journal entries was fun.

Blue was right though. Underhill was more. More color, more oomph, more everything. Rin would blink, and when he opened his eyes again, the sheer wonder of the world around him would hit him. This had to be what a colorblind person felt the first moment they could finally see color. At least, that was the best analogy Rin could come up with.

They were walking down what appeared to be a classic country road. It was dirt-scarred with centuries of tracks from wagons in two parallel paths. The fields to either side were wheat or some other type of tall grass— Rin's farming knowledge was pretty exclusive toward cucumbers and Mama's beans, so he wasn't sure. The grass blew in a gentle wind, rustling pleasantly to the ear. Overhead the sky was cloudless blue, but while the sun shone brilliant yellow, the air was only warm, and Rin didn't have any fear of sunburn.

Ready? Blue asked as he got to his feet. He was in human form, and his broken arm was still held closely to his chest. It wasn't broken any longer, Rin knew, but horses were heavy creatures, and Blue was probably still in danger of rebreaking it if he put his full weight on it.

Blue was damned lucky he had a human form to heal in, but Rin wished he understood the healing magic in his blood better in order to get Blue back to full strength quicker.

Rin stood up, too, and took a second to brush dirt off the seat of his pants before grabbing the backpack and sliding his arms through the straps.

"How much farther do you think it is?" Rin asked as he fell into step at Blue's side. Blue wasn't letting them get more than a foot apart, which Rin understood after Blue's last journal entry. One wrong step, and Rin could accidentally end up somewhere in Underhill where Blue would never find him again.

Jim's house is only a bit farther. Try to fix the idea in your mind that you want to travel to Jim's house. Your mind keeps wandering, and Underhill is having trouble getting us there.

"Sorry, Blue."

I wasn't much better my first few times here. Blue grinned at Rin. *I'll get us there. It'll just take a bit longer.*

They walked on, and Rin tried to think only of Jim's house. Blue had said it was a mansion, but what would a mansion look like in Underhill? Maybe it was built of stone like a medieval castle? Or maybe it was gigantic like the billionaires' houses they sometimes showed on TV. It had to have a lake since Blue had stayed there for a while.

How long was "a while," anyway? Blue had said he'd stayed with Jim for a long time, but as far as Rin could tell, time didn't seem to change his surroundings at all. The sun hadn't moved in the sky, and they had been walking for hours.

What if some of the stories of magic he had heard from books and TV shows were true? Would he return to the human world to find a hundred years had gone by in the hours or days he had been Underhill, or would he return only moments after he and Blue had stepped into the mushroom circle, aged from their time Underhill while the real world hadn't turned?

No, he had to keep thinking about Jim's house. Keeping focused on a destination was the only way to get somewhere in Underhill.

"Blue, if all we need to do is think about somewhere and Underhill will get us there, why can't we think about going to Mama?"

Blue let out a whinny of laughter. *Nothing is that easy. Maybe we could walk to Mama that way, but we're as likely to get to a place she's recently been instead of actually to her. Sometimes when you're searching for a person, you'll end up at their favorite place, somewhere they visit often, but not anywhere near where they really are. There are also spells that keep people from being found, which I'm sure they're using.*

"So how are we going to find Mama?" Rin asked, feeling his limited hope drop to the bottom of his stomach like a lead weight. Jim had been so certain they could find her in this alien place, but so far, they couldn't even get to Jim's house.

With something that can beat those spells and overcome Underhill's tricks, Blue replied cheekily. *Here we are!*

Rin looked away from Blue and saw a house had appeared as they turned a bend. It had been hidden in the long grass, but now Rin could see it wasn't a castle or a massive mansion.

Jim's house wasn't quite double the size of Mama's. It had shingle siding in light gray and a dark-black roof. Wide, inviting windows framed the front door, and a large lake behind the house made it look even more picturesque.

Now that they could see their destination, it felt much quicker to walk the last yards until they reached the front door. It opened as they approached, and a small woman who was maybe four feet tall with a pair of orange-and-black painted butterfly wings on her back stepped out to greet them.

"Blue," she said. Her voice rang like a wind chime. "It's been so long. What brings you here when the Master is out?"

Jim sent me to borrow one of his puppies, Blue explained. Rin nodded to show he agreed even though he had no idea what Blue meant.

"Of course. They're around back." She shut the door and stepped off the dirt path that was the front walk and onto the mown grass encircling the house. Rin and Blue followed her around to the backyard, where there were a number of outbuildings. She pointed at one, then ducked her head and scurried around them to go back inside.

Blue continued to the outbuilding without reacting to her odd behavior. Rin tried not to notice too, but he was curious. What was she? She also hadn't introduced herself to Rin or even looked at him.

Rin had to ask. "Who was that?"

She works for Jim. I think he saved her life from something bad, so she serves him until her life debt is paid. Rin opened his mouth to ask more, but Blue continued speaking before Rin could get the words out. *You don't ask for someone's name in Underhill. It's very rude. If someone wants you to know their name, they'll tell you. She never told me hers.*

Blue knocked on the outbuilding's door. *Hello?* he called.

A chorus of barking started up from what sounded like a dozen dogs. It was so loud the outbuilding seemed to shake with it. A flap set in the door swung open, nearly hitting Blue in the knees, and four very black dogs tumbled outside. All four of them barked for a few more moments until they actually looked to see who they were barking at. When they saw Blue, their long tails began to wag, and their barks became happy chuffs. Their ears were red, Rin saw, as one rolled onto its back in the grass in front of Blue, then hopped back to his feet.

It's nice to see you too. Is your mama around?

The dog nodded and pointed his nose toward the outbuilding. The other three dogs had run off without him, so the dog spun on his paws and ran off without saying goodbye. Blue walked to the door, knocked again to be polite, then pulled it open.

"What are they?" Rin asked softly as he followed Blue into the dim outbuilding.

Cŵn Annwn. Hellhounds in English. Sometimes they're called a Grim. They're friendly enough, and they're great trackers. Their noses were made for the hunt. Blue grinned over his shoulder at Rin but returned his focus to the dog he had stopped in front of.

The dog was a hundred to a hundred and fifty pounds, easily the size of a miniature pony, and when she grinned up at Blue from where she was lying on the ground, every sharp tooth in her wide mouth became visible. Her fur was black, except for her ears, which were a brilliant shade of red.

Nose? Her mental voice was low and growly, but she seemed friendly enough. That wouldn't make Rin step any closer, of course, but it lessened his urge to run outside.

Yes, I need to borrow one of your children. One with a good nose that can track a human hidden somewhere Underhill.

Aodh, she replied. A dog stepped into view from deeper into the outbuilding, no doubt summoned by his name. He was equally as dark and intimidating if still slightly smaller than his mother.

Hunt, Aodh said eagerly.

A good hunt, Blue replied in agreement.

The mother dog shifted slightly, and three puppies appeared, sucking hungrily at her belly—although Rin had never seen puppies the size of watermelons before. A fourth, and probably the reason she had moved, was trying to force his way between the other pups, climbing ineffectually and crying as he tried to get to food. There was an open teat, but the other dogs were so big and the little puppy so much smaller, it couldn't get to it. The puppy was also pale white, unlike every other dog in Rin had seen that day. His ears were as red as the rest though.

Rin couldn't stand by watching. He glanced over at Blue quickly to make certain it was okay, and then over at the mother dog when Blue just grinned at him. When the mother didn't say anything to stop him, Rin tentatively stepped close to pick up the tiny pup. He carefully pushed two of the bigger dogs apart so there was enough room and put the puppy down where it could easily reach his breakfast.

Wean soon, the mama dog said with a heavy sigh that spoke of long suffering.

Hunt first, Aodh cut in insistently. *What hunt?*

His mama was taken, Blue explained, pointing toward Rin as Rin stepped away from the dogs and back to Blue's side. *We need to rescue her and bring her back to the human world.*

Aodh chuffed. *Easy. Go now?*

"Can we go now? The faster we save her, the sooner we can tell Wesley where to shove it," Rin asked eagerly.

No point in staying here, Blue agreed. *What do you need to find her?* Blue asked Aodh.

Sniff her. He smell like her? Aodh pointed his nose at Rin.

He should. He's her son.

Aodh barked softly in reply and walked over to Rin. He was so big that his nose was even with Rin's chest. All he had to do was lean forward to take a big, whuffling sniff. Aodh threw his head back and let out a deafening howl that echoed through the outbuilding. Other howls responded, but Aodh was the only dog that bounded out the door and into the clipped grass outside.

Hurry, Rin! Blue called. He grabbed Rin's hand as he ran after Aodh, no doubt remembering that getting separated would be bad. Rin ran with Blue, holding on to Blue's hand with all his strength.

They rushed onto the grass. Aodh was already heading around the main building toward the dirt path through the tall grass. Rin and Blue sprinted after him, desperately trying to keep him in sight.

They were moving so swiftly, the grass seemed to warp around them, or maybe it was the opposite: Underhill was moving so quickly at the behest of Aodh that the colors streamed past them like a swift-current river. They ran for only five minutes, which was about four minutes longer than Rin had the stamina for, and stopped abruptly in the high grass.

Rin gasped and panted for breath, his free hand pressed to one knee to keep him upright. Blue wasn't out of breath at all, of course, and Aodh was looking at Rin in contempt.

Shh, he said sharply.

Rin tried to breathe softer, taking longer breaths to stop panting, and eventually straightened until he was standing upright again.

Aodh poked his nose through the tall grass, revealing through the space he made that they were at the very edge of the grassy area. The ground was stone-flagged ahead of them, and Rin could see the buildings of a small town. This looked exactly like how the movies portrayed a medieval setting, with stone and wood houses, thatched roofs, and sheep and chickens roaming freely through the streets. Aodh pulled back before Rin could get a good look.

At inn, he said.

They're probably keeping her in a room there, Blue said in agreement. *We need to figure out which room and then go rescue her.*

"How do we do that?" Rin asked, his voice the softest whisper he could make it.

This is a sidhe village, Blue explained. *You're part sidhe, so you can walk in. Aodh and I won't be welcome.*

He pulled Rin around gently so he could rummage in the pack on Rin's back. When he turned Rin back around, he was holding out a small leather pouch.

Go to the inn and sit at the bar. Order something to drink, but don't drink it! he warned sternly. *See if you can find Mama. Aodh and I will sneak in the back door and try to search upstairs.*

"How will I find you if I've got Mama?" Rin asked.

Aodh can find you anywhere. Go to Jim's house. Keep the picture of his house in your mind, and Underhill will get you there. I'll meet you. Blue bent forward and pressed their lips together quickly. He whinnied softly as he pulled away. *Go.*

Rin went, stepping out of the grass and onto the stone cobbles of the street. There were a dozen buildings nearby. Each one had writing on them, so this had to be a shopping area, but Rin couldn't read the language. He did recognize the picture of a steaming bowl of soup and a flagon of some sort of alcohol on a sign hanging from one of the larger buildings. He took a deep breath at the door to brace himself, then pushed the door open and stepped inside.

There were about a dozen or so people inside, some sitting at the round tables together and others sitting alone at a table or at the long bar that took up the entire right-hand wall. The room was large enough to hold three times that amount of people.

Mama was sitting at a round table in the far-left corner with two men sitting on either side of her, boxing her in. Her eyes widened when she saw Rin, but she kept her mouth firmly shut. Rin found an empty barstool to sit on before his knees collapsed.

She was alive, and she didn't look hurt. Instead she looked furious, like she was just waiting for the perfect moment to give the men what for, and the relief in knowing she was okay lifted a heavy weight from Rin's shoulders. Now he had to figure out how to rescue her and get away safe.

"You need a room or passing through?" a man asked as he ambled over to Rin from the employee side of the bar. He was tall and thin like Jim and his ears were pointed, but the similarities ended there. The man was so pale-skinned Rin was surprised he couldn't see through him to the bones and muscles inside, and his eyes were huge in his face.

"Just a drink before I get on the road again," Rin replied, hastily remembering not to say thank you. He reached into the pouch Blue had given him, pulled out two of the smaller coins he could feel inside, and put them on the bar. The coins vanished, and a moment later a wooden mug filled with an amber liquid that reeked of alcohol appeared in its place.

Rin didn't touch the mug, just stared at it as if the answer to how to save Mama would appear on the surface of his drink. He glanced over his shoulder again, trying to act like he was simply looking around the room for someone to sit with. One of the men with Mama was tall and thin with pointed ears and lightly tanned skin. The other man was large and fat, but it was the type of fat that hardened into muscle. Mama was looking at the table, frowning in thought. Maybe she could think of a way to get free. All they needed to do was get outside, and hopefully, Underhill would get them to safety.

Before he could come up with a plan, the front door slammed. "I thought I smelled the vile stench of one of Dian Cecht's brood," a woman's voice snapped from behind Rin. He looked around in alarm. She could only mean him. "You think yourself safe from my retribution out here, far from your ancestral lands? More fool you!" Her voice was a deep Irish brogue, yet at the same time she didn't sound like any Irish Rin had ever heard. She was probably speaking like the Irish had spoken four hundred years ago, before their shores had been invaded and their heritage destroyed.

"You're the fool"—a man called as he stood from his table—"if you think that where Dian Cecht walks, those that support him will not also be nearby. The great healer can call for aid in any town thanks to his healing of King Nuada."

"Political parlor tricks," the woman scoffed. "Give Nuada the pretender back his arm and look what Dian Cecht reaped in return. Lands enough that his children did not fight for their inheritance, power to call for the army's support whenever he wishes, and the ear of the king for all matters big and small. Dian Cecht might as well be king, for all Nuada granted him, and I will support neither pretender."

Both of the men guarding Mama had stood when the woman and man had started arguing. They were a full step away from the table, eagerly watching the budding fight.

"I will have his head for my trophy!" the woman finished, pointing at Rin. Her hand was glowing, and Rin dove for the floor with a yelp barely in time to avoid the streak of light aimed for his head.

"You dare!" the man roared. He began growing, losing his glamor and revealing an eight-foot-tall body with shoulders and hips wide enough to match that height. He lunged for the woman, a short sword suddenly appearing in each hand.

Rin rolled desperately as the woman fired off another shot before she had to turn her attention to her attacker. The rest of the people in the inn drew close to observe, as if the fight was a spectator sport. Even the two men guarding Mama drifted forward a few more steps.

As Rin watched from the floor where he was crouched, Mama slithered low in her chair until she slipped under the table. She crawled behind one of her guards and headed for the back door. Rin crept after her, hoping the tingling at the back of his neck was nerves rather than another attack.

The floor shook as the large man fell hard. The woman's cackle of glee stopped a moment later when he recovered. Rin inched forward faster. He looked up to see one of Mama's guards grinning at him in a way that said he was enjoying Rin's suffering. Fine, he could keep watching Rin, Rin told his roiling stomach, as long as he didn't notice Mama was gone until after they were safely out the back door.

Mama made it through the doorway faster than Rin since she was closer, but Rin scrambled through a few moments later. He stumbled to his feet in time to hear two new roars. The guards had finally noticed.

"Run!" he yelled. He grabbed Mama's hand and held it tight so they wouldn't get separated in Underhill.

They were in the kitchen. A roaring fireplace was to Rin's right, and a long table filled the center of the room. They ran around the table and headed for the door on the other side. They reached it just as the guards rushed into the room.

The guards didn't bother running around the table. The big one waved his hand, and the table vanished with a concussive boom. Rin flew through the doorway, shards of wood slicing through the air around him, and hit the stone ground outside with a hard thud. He had inadvertently let go of Mama's hand, and he scrambled to roll over, coughing hard with his ears ringing and his eyes watering. Mama was struggling to roll over, one hand pressed to her weak hip with a grimace of pain on her face.

Heal! Rin urged as he hurried on hands and knees to her side. *Heal!* They couldn't run if Mama's hip was hurting again, and they had to run into the grass if they were going to escape into Underhill.

Rin pressed his hand over Mama's, and a flash of light blossomed underneath his palm. Mama let out a gasp of relief, then gaped at him for a brief second before a yell from inside the building brought back their senses.

"Let's go." Mama stood and pulled Rin up.

Go now! Blue's voice sounded. A roaring whinny came from inside the kitchen. *We'll hold them off until you get safe.*

"Blue!" Rin screamed. Mama was pulling him toward the grass, but his feet had stopped moving at the noise from Blue.

"As if those two idiots can stop a kelpie at full druther," Mama scolded, yanking on Rin's arm insistently. "He won't run to safety until he knows you're far enough away. Let's go, Rin. Now."

Mama was right, Rin knew that, but everything inside him wanted to be at Blue's side, helping Blue stay alive.

"Now, Rin," Mama repeated sternly, with another yank.

Rin swallowed back a sob and turned, running with Mama. Aodh's echoing howl followed them as they ran.

"Think of Jim's house," Rin told Mama as they reached the grass. His voice cracked as tears wet his cheeks, but he kept on moving. Rin forced Blue out of his head and pictured the gray shingle siding and black roof, the outbuilding full of massive dogs, and the lake that had kept Blue alive for however long. "Don't think of anything else except Jim's house," he repeated.

They ran through the grass, pushing through the tall stalks with their free hands since Rin was making certain not to let go of Mama. Underhill wasn't streaming around them without Aodh's help, but somehow Rin felt like they were still moving quickly from the village on a path Mama's guards would have a hard time following.

They had to get to Jim's house, where it would be safe, and Blue had to be there waiting for him. Yes, with Aodh's help, Blue could get there well before Mama and Rin. Rin was heading toward Blue, to Jim's house.

Rin and Mama kept moving. They slowed to a fast walk for a while to catch their breath and because every bit of Rin was aching from being blasted through the kitchen doorway. They returned to jogging when they could. The only time they stopped was for a brief moment to drink some water from the bottles in the backpack Rin had somehow managed not to drop.

There was no way to tell how long they had been running, but as long as there weren't any sounds of pursuit behind them, it didn't matter how long it took to get to Jim's house and safety. Rin did his best to keep his picture of Jim's house in the forefront of his mind and led the way so Mama's scattered thoughts wouldn't confuse Underhill. He wasn't following a path, but he hoped Underhill was still steering them correctly.

Rin pushed past more tall grass, and his feet stumbled onto carefully clipped grass. Rin fell to his knees with a startled cry. He looked up and saw the lake and the outbuildings. Somehow, they had reached the house.

"Took you long enough," the woman with the wings snapped, suddenly appearing in front of Rin and Mama. "I've had a bath and a bed waiting for hours while you've been lazing your way over here."

She grabbed Mama's free hand, then waited impatiently while Mama stared at her.

"Come on," the woman grumbled. Mama glanced at Rin.

"She works for Jim. This is his house in Underhill," Rin explained. He turned to the woman and added, "You'll keep Mama safe?"

"She has to come into the house first. I can't protect her out here, and the brownie family that keeps the house won't venture outside either." The woman scowled at their clasped hands and lifted one eyebrow pointedly at Mama.

"Go with her," Rin said to Mama. "I'm going to wait for Blue."

Mama nodded and smiled sadly at him. "Thanks for coming for me, Rin." She let go of his hand and pulled him into a hug, then kissed him softly on the cheek before leaving him to wait for Blue. Rin watched as she followed the woman with the butterfly wings around the house and out of sight before he turned to look for Blue.

There was no guarantee Blue would come out of the grass in the same place as Rin. It would be better to move to the center of the lawn where he could see more. He stopped walking at the shore of the lake and sank down onto the sandy bank.

He trailed his fingers in the cool water, trying not to think of Blue's roaring whinny, hoping it wasn't pain he had heard in Blue's voice. No, he was making that up. Blue had simply been desperate to give Rin enough time to escape, and Rin shouldn't let his frightened imagination run wild.

The water was getting difficult to see in front of him. At first, Rin thought he had been crying too much, but he wiped his eyes on his sleeve and looked up, only to realize the sun was actually setting. The sky was full of brilliant pinks and oranges, shading up to purple in the east. It was the most beautiful sunset Rin had ever seen, and for a moment it distracted him from the worry twisting his gut.

A muffled woof sounded behind him, and Rin jumped in surprise and spun around, hope rising in his chest for a second before he saw the black mama dog standing behind him. There was something in her mouth, and she bent forward to drop it in Rin's lap.

Yours, now, she said, adding a woof to her words before heading back to the outbuilding on silent paws. Rin looked down at the tiny white puppy squirming around in his lap. The puppy yawned, showing off teeth that looked really sharp, and then tucked its nose under its tail and went to sleep.

Rin wished he dared sleep. Every bone and muscle ached, and he was certain his entire back was one giant bruise. There were scratches on his arms and face from the wooden table explosion, and he felt sticky with sweat and blood. But Blue was still out there somewhere.

If Blue didn't return by the time the sun rose again, Rin would ask the mama dog if another of her children was interested in going to search for Blue and Aodh. For now, he returned to staring at the lake, hoping with everything in his heart that Blue was okay.

*

Such pain, child.

The voice was strangely familiar to Rin. It was a man's voice, low yet compassionate.

No child of mine should suffer as you have suffered. I did not know your mother was with child when I left, and by the time I returned, she had vanished. Years I have lost in your upbringing, but I see within you the strength of your heritage. Your mother was strong, and I, your father, am stronger still. Look within my power, see what you can learn, and heal your body with the skills I should have taught you from your birth until now.

Suddenly, Rin was surrounded by bright light. Images flashed through the light, almost faster than Rin could make each one out. He could see a glowing hand here pressing against a gaping, bloody wound. And the wound vanished. There, a missing arm, arteries gushing with the pulse of the heart, and a bucket of water quickly drawn from a glowing well. The severed arm pressed against the shoulder and water poured over the seam, and the arm was attached again. Now disease, a terrible cough, blisters, boils, fever, and a cloth gently pressed to the brow to call away the malady.

There is great power in the hands of the children of Dian Cecht. I see you have begun to learn on your own how to heal your own broken body and the breaks of others. Watch, my child. Learn all you should have known.

There were more images, terrible images, because the ability to heal also came with the ability to kill. It was so easy to stop a heart or to cause disease. A touch here, a brush there, and bodies lay in his wake. Rin shuddered.

Yes, there is great responsibility in this power. You must always temper your hatred and fear with happiness and love, or you will fall to the unseelie ways of the power. And you know love.

"Blue," Rin gasped. "I can't find Blue."

Hush, child. I have seen to Blue. That a child of mine would lie with a lesser fae...well, you were brought up without the proper niceties in life. I can feel how strongly you yearn for him; your heart beats for your Blue, does it not? Love, perhaps, overcomes the differences in your species. I will have to ponder on that idea for a while, but I shall do my best to accept your union. Now, wake, my child, and tend to your Blue.

*

Rin sat up slowly, blinking sleep out of his eyes and wondering when he had fallen asleep. How had he fallen asleep when at any moment Blue could need his help? And his dream had been so strange...

The sky in the east was beginning to lighten. Either nights weren't as long as days in Underhill, or he had been sleeping for hours. He looked around, hoping to see Blue nearby, waiting for him to wake up, but he was still alone, aside from the puppy snuffling happily in his lap.

Except...there! There was something moving in the tall grass. The rustling noise of someone pushing it aside was plain in the quiet of the dawn. He carefully placed the puppy to one side, and then leapt to his feet.

It had to be Blue. It had to be. There was no way the guards or the woman who had tried to kill Rin had followed him here. He hurried across the clipped lawn toward the grass. It was only after a few steps that he realized all his bruises were gone.

That realization was wiped from his mind when Aodh limped out of the grass, his front right paw held up in the air as he fought not to put weight on it. Right behind him was Blue, who looked tired, but okay.

Rin! Blue whinnied. *I was so scared! What if I never found you!*

Would have found, Aodh disagreed, sounding as tired as Blue looked.

"Are you okay? What happened?" Rin asked, trying not to crowd Blue even as he desperately wanted to jump into Blue's arms and hold him close.

I broke my arm again, Blue said grumpily, *but once Aodh felt that you and Mama had escaped, we ran for it. Except I think we ran in the opposite direction of Jim's place, and it took a while for Underhill to figure out where we meant to go. And we were moving slow 'cause of our injuries.*

Now that Rin knew what to look for, Blue's arm did have a funny-looking bump under the skin. Rin knew how to handle that. He reached inside himself, exactly as his dream had taught him, and pulled free some magic from his core. As he touched Blue, who sighed and happily curled into Rin's arms, a flare of light flashed between them.

What was... The break's gone? Rin, my arm's fixed. How'd you do that?

"I dreamed my father was here," Rin said slowly, trying to parse through what he remembered from his dream. "He showed me all sorts of things I can do with my power. And then I woke up just in time for you to finally get back here."

Rin kept his arm around Blue's waist, unwilling to let Blue go now that he had Blue in his arms again, but he bent down as he called up more magic, and a touch to Aodh's fur caused another flash of light. Aodh let out a relieved sigh and put his hurt paw down on the ground again.

Better. Aodh let out a yawn. *Sleep now. Had fun hunting.* He trotted off toward the dogs' outbuilding.

That's how you say thanks in Underhill, Blue explained. He let out a wide, jaw-cracking yawn, then neighed softly into Rin's shoulder where he was tiredly resting his head. *We should get home soon. I don't want to sleep here. Where's Mama so we can go?*

"Mama's in the house. Let's go knock and see if she's ready to leave." Rin was about to walk toward the house when a pointed yip sounded from near his feet. He looked down to see the puppy grinning at him.

Uh-oh. Did it get attached to you? Blue snarled gently at the puppy as if to tell it to go away. The puppy simply yipped happily in reply.

"One of the other dogs dropped it off earlier, said it was mine now?" Rin said, asking Blue to clarify.

It got attached. Hope Mama doesn't mind dogs. Pick it up so we can go. You'll have to name it, but it should be house-trained. The last was said pointedly to the puppy, who gave Blue a disgusted look as if to say of course he was house-trained.

Rin obeyed, bending down to pick up the puppy, which curled up in Rin's arms. They walked up toward the house together, Blue still practically draped over Rin like an exhausted blanket.

Mama was waiting at the door, but there was no sign of the other woman anywhere.

"About time," she said sharply, but with a relieved smile for Rin and Blue. "How do we get out of here?"

Getting out of Underhill is easy. You just have to know how to orient yourself so you don't end up halfway across the human world, Blue explained. *Grab hold and I'll get us out.*

Rin quickly repeated Blue's words for Mama, who didn't waste any time gripping Rin's free shoulder. Blue let out a soft whinny, and the world blurred around them for a moment before the familiar house and barn materialized as they appeared in the middle of the front yard. It was dark out, but the sudden flare of light in the house as the kitchen light was turned on said that Jim was still awake.

"Get a shower and get some sleep, and for goodness sake put that puppy down now," Mama instructed as the front door was flung open and Jim ran out into the yard. "In the morning we're going to have to give that damned Wesley a little what-for."

She strode forward to meet Jim halfway. Rin didn't look, instead dragging an increasingly heavy Blue into the house, up the stairs, and into the bathroom for a quick rinse before they fell into bed together.

Chapter Six

"You were gone for two days," Jim explained over breakfast the next morning. Mama was making pancakes again, and Blue was happily eying the bottle of syrup sitting in the middle of the table. "I got the roof repaired on the house and the barn and did some digging on what's been going on in Underhill that might have caused all this. Turns out, Dian Cecht and Nuada are close confidants these days. Dian Cecht did fix Nuada's arm, and then Miach finished the healing, which allowed Nuada to retake the throne. That gave Dian Cecht an unprecedented amount of power and influence even in the seelie court. Of course, that hasn't made some of the other courtiers happy. A number of fae have noticed Rin and put two and two together, and I believe one of them has the ear of a seelie who wants to remove Dian Cecht from power and was willing to ally themselves with Wesley."

"Like the woman who attacked me at the bar, saying she wanted to kill me because I was a member of Dian Cecht's family?" Rin asked.

"Most likely," Jim replied with a nod of agreement. "Most seelie sidhe won't come to the human world. They'll send lesser fae instead, but most lesser fae aren't strong enough to tangle with a kelpie, even a young kelpie like Blue."

Blue preened, neighing happily as he grinned at Rin.

"But Wesley might not even know Underhill exists. They may have approached him under human guise and offered him a way to destroy Lizzy that would allow them to get to Rin and therefore get to Dian Cecht. My guess is they were hoping Blue and I would go Underhill for the rescue, leaving Rin here unprotected. It seems like we might have outsmarted them. Now we need to stay a step ahead."

"Wesley gave us three days to ship the horses to him. It's now day three," Rin said slowly, trying to think through their options. "Do you think he knows Mama's been rescued?"

"If that bastard shows up here..." Mama snarled from where she was sliding the last few pancakes onto a plate. She joined them at the table and sat, dropping the plate onto the center of the table with an angry plunk.

"He very well might," Jim replied with a shrug. "But we're ready for him this time. Between Blue and me, we'll be able to fight off anything he tries."

I'll crunch his bones, Blue agreed eagerly as he took three pancakes off the plate and began to drown them in syrup.

"We can't kill him, Blue," Rin gasped, his hand pausing in the air on its way to the pancakes.

"It's bad enough we've got vindictive seelies trying to capture us," Mama groused. "Last thing we need is the human law looking at us too."

Rin took some pancakes and rescued the syrup from Blue so he could drown his own plate. He was hungry after the last two days of eating only the nonperishable travel crap he and Blue had stuffed in the backpack, and Rin was honestly used to Blue talking about crunching all sorts of things at this point, so as soon as there was enough syrup on his plate, Rin started stuffing his face. Mama irritably snatched what was left of the syrup bottle from him.

"I think we should wait and see if Wesley shows up here," Rin said once half his pancakes were gone. "Maybe he'll crawl back into the hole he came out of when he realizes Mama got away safe."

Maybe pigs fly.

Rin grinned at Blue, who also smiled.

Jim rolled his eyes. "Ineloquent, but true. Wesley will be here sometime today. I have no doubt about that. The question is, who or what will he bring with him?"

"I'll be bringing my shotgun," Mama cut in firmly. "They'll see what happens to them if they try lighting my house on fire again."

My arm's better now, so I can run really fast and hit them really hard. Since I'm not allowed to crunch bones, Blue grumbled.

"No bone crunching, please," Rin replied even as Jim was rolling his eyes again.

"I have a few interesting trap spells I've been dying to use," Jim added between bites of his own pancakes. "Lizzy, did I ever mention how wonderfully you cook?"

"It's nice to hear someone appreciates my efforts," Mama said with a pointed look at Rin and Blue.

"Aww, Mama," Rin said with a pout.

"Go get in the shower, boys," Mama continued with a grin for them. "The barn still needs to be mucked and swept. Chores don't stop just because an idiot might be attacking today."

"Yes, Mama," Rin replied obediently. Blue let out a heavy, whuffling sigh but nodded as well.

"And your puppy ran off into the pasture this morning. Jim assures me he'll be back on his own, but keep an eye out for him when you're outside."

Rin cleared his plate and headed upstairs to shower, Blue right behind him. Only once they were safely enclosed in the privacy of the bathroom did Rin abruptly spin around and pull Blue tightly into his arms.

I'm still okay, Rin, Blue insisted gently, even as his own arms were strongly holding Rin close. *You healed my broken bone, and we found each other again. Underhill didn't defeat us, and today we'll win over everything that dares threaten us. It'll be okay.*

"You can't know that," Rin said, his voice muffled against Blue's shoulder.

I'm going to do everything I can to make sure that's the truth. That's what matters. Will you promise to stay safe? Blue asked. His nose nuzzled into Rin's hair, and he was neighing softly almost like a cat purring.

"I don't know how to fight," Rin said as an answer. Mama had made certain Rin knew his way around a gun since she didn't want him to accidentally shoot himself, but he wasn't any sort of marksman. Thanks to his legs, he hadn't ever taken martial arts. In fact, the only way he knew how to fight was the ways his father had shown him in that dream, except those ways led to unseelie, and Rin honestly didn't feel comfortable purposefully making someone sick. "But I do know how to heal. If anyone gets hurt, I'm going to come help."

Blue sighed, his breath ruffling through Rin's hair. *I understand. Just remember, you're my favorite snack, and I'll be very sad if you get hurt too.*

"I know, Blue. Thanks." Rin slowly pulled away, not wanting to leave the warmth and much-needed comfort of Blue's arms, yet knowing the last thing he wanted was to still be in the shower when Wesley decided to show up.

It took a few seconds for the water to warm up. Rin stripped out of his pajamas and hopped in. Blue got into the tub with him and gently pulled the shampoo out of Rin's hands.

Let me, my pretty snack.

*

Showering took longer than expected for reasons Rin didn't want to have to explain to Mama. He hurried through the house, still damp, but in clean jeans and a T-shirt, Blue right on his heels. They made it outside, across the yard, and into the barn without being spotted.

"I think we should put Demon in an adjacent stall," Rin said as they strode down the walkway between the loose box stalls on either side. "We can clean out his stall and get him back inside faster that way."

I'll get a harness, Blue called as he hurried past Rin toward the back of the barn where they kept their tack. Rin followed because the pitchfork and wheelbarrow he needed were back there too. Except Blue had stopped walking outside Demon's box, and both Demon and Blue had their heads cocked to the side as if they could hear something. Rin froze in place to listen too, but he didn't hear anything.

Stay in the barn, Blue said firmly to Rin. He pressed one hand to Rin's shoulder before he walked back to the entrance. Rin still couldn't hear anything. He walked to the entrance too, but as instructed, remained inside. Blue went directly to the middle of the yard and stood with his hands braced on his hips, staring not at the road like Rin expected, but instead down the hoof-scarred path leading past his lake and eventually to the forest.

The forest was glowing.

Rin blinked a few times to double-check, and the yellowish glow that enveloped the trees didn't change.

"What is it?" Rin called to Blue.

Blue didn't answer, all of his focus no doubt directed at whatever was causing the glow. Jim walked out of the house and went to join Blue in the yard.

"A sidhe of some power is attempting to leave Underhill, and they apparently don't know how to use a mushroom circle," Jim explained without looking away from the forest. "It takes power to force a doorway to open instead of simply using properly willed intent as you would with a circle."

"What does that mean for us?" Rin asked.

Bad, bad, bad things, Blue replied, his voice shaking slightly, which had Rin's stomach jumping up into his chest in worry.

Jim continued explaining since Blue wasn't being particularly descriptive at the moment. "I think I told you at breakfast, most sidhe don't leave Underhill. They send lesser fae to do their bidding instead. Sometimes they'll send less powerful sidhe, but they never come themselves. They, therefore, never have cause to learn about a circle and have to force their way out if they ever do decide to leave."

Rin wanted to ask who was coming, but the words got stuck in his throat. They weren't prepared to fight a powerful sidhe. Not by a long shot.

The window in the sitting room next to the front door was pushed upward, and Mama's worried face looked out into the yard before she stepped back and leveled her favorite shotgun out through the opening instead. Rin stepped back from the center of the open barn doors and tucked his body behind one of the jambs so he could still see out into the yard but wouldn't be an easy target.

The sudden crunch of tires on the drive made him jump in surprise, and Blue and Jim spun to face the oncoming car. Blue's human glamor snapped into place just as a pickup truck with a large horse trailer attached pulled into view. Wesley parked and jumped out of the cab, his usual smarmy grin already in place.

"I thought I would make it easier on you if I came and took the horses myself since it looks like you're too lazy to bring them on your own. Don't you care what happens to Lizzy?" Wesley sounded genuinely curious as he glanced around the yard. Then he saw Mama grinning cheekily at him from behind the double barrels of the shotgun she had pointed right at his oversized head. He took a step back as if he was about to make a run for the safety of his car, but then the car's passenger-side door opened.

"Now, now," a man's voice said softly and very gently. "There is no need for violence. Please, put the gun down. Let us talk it over like civilized creatures." His voice had a beat to it, a gentle, hypnotic cadence that somehow made Rin want to step out of the barn and walk right up to him.

There was no way he was human. Rin shook his head, trying to get the words reverberating through his brain out. He plucked at a bit of his magic, wondering if he could shield himself from the magic in the man's words. Mama's gun hadn't moved an inch, but then Mama was stubborn as a mule and even less likely to obey someone's sweet words than Blue was.

"Are you done?" Jim asked sharply after a long, pointed moment in which no one moved.

The stranger said Jim's name, or what Rin thought was Jim's name. He had never heard "Jim" take four syllables to say before, but Rin also didn't think "Jim" was a sidhe name. It was probably a nickname instead.

"How surprising to see you here," the stranger continued. "I had heard a rumor you were consorting with a human. How base of you."

The name Jim said in reply took five syllables and was equally as incomprehensible to Rin's ears. His English abilities parsed it down to something like Claire.

"Which faction do you support?" Jim asked Claire. "I assume it's one of the ones looking to topple Nuada from the seelie throne."

"Civil war is inevitable," Claire replied, and though his voice remained calm, for some reason Rin thought he heard snakes hissing among his words. "Nuada cannot contain it, and we will bring Dian Cecht to his knees when we kidnap his offspring."

Jim scoffed. "I don't know if you remember your history at all, but Dian Cecht killed his son Miach when

Miach upstaged him in healing Nuada's arm. Blackmailing Dian Cecht that way is pointless."

"Fool." Claire laughed. "Miach asked to leave Underhill. He wanted to explore the other realms without the burden of his father's power tying him to responsibilities in Underhill. Everyone knows this, and if you don't believe me, then why have you been consorting with Miach's youngest son?" Claire pointed toward the barn door where Rin was hiding. "I will have the child now, or I will kill you first and still take the child."

Jim was already shaking his head no in answer, but Blue was the one who spoke first.

He is mine! I won't let you have him! He let out an aggressive whinny full of the promise of sharp hooves impacting in tender places.

Claire glanced at Blue briefly, then dismissed him and refocused on Jim. Clearly, Claire was an idiot.

Blue growled low, and his glamor faded away. He didn't turn into his horse form; he remained human, but it was his most magical-looking shape in human form. He had horns and claws, and even the air around him seemed to be shaded slightly blue.

"I'm afraid Blue is correct. We will not be giving anyone to you," Jim reiterated firmly. His glamor didn't change, yet the way he was looking at Claire said he was as ready as Blue.

"Too bad," Claire said, but from his grin Rin could tell Claire was excited by the prospect of a fight.

The wind suddenly picked up outside, the dirt from the yard blowing against Jim's and Blue's ankles and swirling through the barns. Little dust devils spun around, grabbing stray hay to fling at the house before they dissipated.

"He's a sylph," Jim growled. His shoulders flexed, and a whip of magic flew at Claire, who batted it aside with a gust of air and a laugh.

"The strongest sylph in Underhill," Claire crowed in agreement. "Now give me the child!"

The air blew harder, rattling the open, heavy barn doors against the side of the barn. It blew in Rin's face, and he had to shield his eyes from the dirt. When the wind left him, it took all the air around him with it.

Rin tried to gasp for breath, but there wasn't anything to breathe. He stumbled away from his hiding place, hoping to find another patch of air, but there was nothing anywhere.

Rin! Blue screeched. Water splashed in Rin's face, but his eyes were streaming and his lungs burning; he didn't have the energy to see what Blue was doing. He fell to his knees, still desperately trying to find any air at all.

The shotgun went off, a bang Rin only vaguely heard through the rushing in his ears. There were sparkles flashing across his eyes, black and rainbow and a terrible omen. His heart was desperately thumping in his burning chest, but there still wasn't any air.

He was going to pass out.

And then what? an inner voice that somehow sounded like Mama's scolding asked him sharply. *You'll let Claire take you to Underhill? What, you're going to wait around for Blue to rescue you when you very well know Blue would die trying?*

No way in hell. Rin gritted his teeth and called on his magic. He knew how to bring breath back to the breathless, how to feed the heart with oxygen to keep it beating and the body alive until the lungs could breathe again. It felt so very wrong inside his body to not have air pumping through his lungs, and he kept on gasping desperately, but the sparkles faded from his vision.

Blue went flying across the yard, pushed by a massive gust of air. His body hit the side of the barn with an awful thud just past where Rin could see through the doorway. Jim had dropped his glamor completely, his horned head and deep-black skin visible as he fired spell after spell at Claire. The shotgun went off a second time. Blue hadn't gotten up.

Rin's magic couldn't sustain him forever—his body needed oxygen, but there still wasn't any air at all around his head—but even more desperately than air, Rin needed to know Blue was alive. He couldn't yell without air and couldn't speak with his mind like Blue. There was only one way to be certain.

His hands and legs were shaking as he carefully stepped out of the barn door. He couldn't say whether that was because he was oxygen-deprived or whether he was deeply afraid of what he was about to see. A few steps past the doorway revealed Blue's body, slumped on the ground. Blue wasn't moving, and Rin wasn't sure whether he was even breathing.

But Blue had to be okay. He had to be.

Rin tried to run, but his starved muscles protested, and he staggered for a moment to catch his balance, wasting precious seconds. He still moved as quickly as he dared and sank to the ground at Blue's side.

His hands were already glowing with power before he gently reached out to touch Blue on the shoulder. The power immediately sank into Blue. Broken ribs—three of them—and the start of a nasty concussion from where his head had hit the barn. Rin would have let out a sigh of relief had he the air, but his body shook free of the knot of worry he had been curled into. Thankfully, none of Blue's injuries were life-threatening, but they were still dangerous enough if not treated properly. Rin let his magic work through Blue, healing the injuries. With each reknitted bone, relief sank into him.

Blue would be okay. That was all that mattered.

Rin? You're okay? Blue's bright eyes blinked open, unfocused as they took in Rin leaning over him. After another blink, his gaze sharpened. *You're not okay. You can't sustain yourself with magic like this!*

Rin wanted to tell Blue he was only doing what he had to in order to stay alive, but Blue seemed to understand him without the words being said aloud. He frowned and let out an angry snarl.

I'll kill him for you, Rin. That'll make his nasty spell stop! Blue gently pushed Rin aside, then stood and ran for where Claire was battling with Jim. Water erupted from the ground around Claire, enveloping him for a brief moment before a gust of air forced the water away. Blue jumped through the gust feet-first, hitting Clair directly in the chest, knocking them both to the ground.

I'll kill you! Blue screamed. *Let my snack go!*

They grappled on the ground, rolling around in the mud and snarling. Blue's sharp claws scored bloody red lines down Claire's arms and chest, but Claire defended himself, somehow keeping Blue's claws away from his throat and face.

The sparkles were returning to the corners of Rin's vision. He had used too much of his magic healing Blue; there wasn't enough left to sustain him. He slumped against the side of the barn, leaning where Blue had been just a few moments ago, and helplessly watched the fight.

He didn't know if he wanted Blue to win the battle. Yes, Rin wanted to live. He wanted to spend many more days with Blue, romping in the shower, mucking out stalls, and swimming in the lake. But he didn't want Claire's death weighing on Blue's conscience for the rest of Blue's life. Rin wasn't worth that type of terrible pain.

There was someone else walking into the yard. Rin reached up to rub his eyes, certain he was seeing an oxygen-starved mirage, but when he lowered his hand, the man was still there. He had come from the other side of the barn where the path to Blue's lake began.

A shot of alarm ran through Rin. They had forgotten about the glowing forest! He struggled to sit up, to try to do anything to warn Blue and Jim and Mama, who had their backs to the man, but his muscles failed him.

The man glanced over at Rin, his light-blue eyes sharp as they took him in, and a frown grew on his face. He turned to look at the fight, still frowning.

"That is enough!"

Rin recognized that firm voice, or a voice very similar to it, actually. It wasn't quite the voice from his dream, but the cadence and tone were so similar.

"My lord!" Jim gasped as he spun around. He immediately bowed low to the man, and stayed bowed, with his back dangerously to Claire and Blue.

"I said, that is enough," the man repeated when neither Blue nor Claire appeared to have heard him.

Blue rolled away with a snarl, pushed by a bit of Claire's air. He was about to jump back into the fray—Blue's leg muscles flexed and his knees bent—but then Blue happened to glance over his shoulder. He froze in place, half crouched to leap but unwilling to move.

Claire hissed when he saw the man but didn't get up from the ground where he was bleeding from dozens of scratches.

"Release my grandson at once," the man said.

Suddenly cool, precious air flooded Rin's face. He gulped it down desperately, breathing so hard and fast he was practically hyperventilating. He let his magic fade with a sense of relief. Air had never tasted so good before, even though it was scented with horse and blood.

Blue unfroze when he saw Rin was breathing again. He trotted around the man in a wide arc, not quite looking up at him as he moved, and sank to the ground at Rin's side. He helped prop Rin up in a sitting position, holding him tightly in a hug Rin couldn't help relaxing into.

"My son had mentioned this bit of interest," the man said as he watched Blue and Rin together. "I will not forbid it."

As if, Blue scoffed, but quietly, as if he only dared let Rin hear.

The man heard anyway. "Yes, well, lesser fae have always been unbiddable."

Rin scowled, but like Blue, he didn't quite dare open his mouth to say anything out loud. The man was oddly scary in a way Rin couldn't quite find the words to explain.

"I admit I had misgivings when my son asked me to leave Underhill to protect my half-human grandson. None of my own half children ever had such a need. But I owed Miach a great boon, so I came. It is unfortunate that Miach was right to send me." He was looking at Claire as he spoke, and his eyes had lost their gentle shade of blue. "I knew there were factions in seelie looking to end the current order of things, but to go so far as to attack innocents? That is unseelie in nature. Claire, to see one such as you fallen so far is truly saddening."

Claire's glare at the man said he wanted to refute that, but like Rin, he couldn't open his mouth.

"Be gone, Claire. Return to Underhill, where you will face seelie justice for your unseelie crimes."

Claire's body began to move, dragging along the ground toward the man. Claire let out a desperate scream, his fingers and toes digging into the earth around him, but nothing he did stopped his forward momentum. He went past Blue and Rin, around the barn, and up the path toward Blue's lake without slowing. Rin could hear his screaming for a few minutes after he was gone from sight.

"My lord," Jim said from where he was still bowing. "Claire worked for a faction looking to unseat King Nuada."

"Rise, Jim. I was aware of those factions, and I had guessed Claire's allegiance given his presence here. It is good to have confirmation. Now, introduce me to my grandson and his kelpie."

Jim rose from his bow, but he didn't move otherwise. "This is Rin Roark and Blue. Rin, Blue, this is Dian Cecht."

I know who you are, Blue huffed. *You saved my snack.* He ran a hand through Rin's hair as he spoke, smiling down at Rin.

"Your thanks is noted, Blue," Dian Cecht replied, his lips tilting upward slightly in an amused grin as he watched them together. "Miach should be here within an hour or so. I will take my leave now that your safety is assured. It was nice to meet you, Rin Roark. Should you and Blue ever have cause to enter Underhill, please come visit me." He nodded to them and Jim, and then headed off after Claire.

A few moments after Dian Cecht left, the front door of the house opened and Mama stomped outside, her shotgun still in her hand.

"Miach's coming here?" she asked sharply, glancing around the yard as if to assess the damage. She would have to get a load of gravel sent up to fix the driveway, but somehow the house and barns had been spared.

"Apparently," Jim replied with a shrug. "Probably just to see Rin, and I doubt he'll stay much longer than his father. Still, it's best to have this mess cleaned up before he arrives." He and Mama both turned to the pickup truck and trailer still sitting in the driveway. Wesley was nowhere in sight.

"Where did that bastard get to?" Mama said with a groan.

"I couldn't keep track of him in the fighting." Jim craned his neck to look around. Rin didn't see Wesley anywhere either, not that he had a great vantage from where he was still sitting.

A yipping sound came from behind the horse trailer, then a growl and a yell of pain. Wesley stumbled into view with Rin's little puppy's teeth dug deep into his ankle.

"Call him off, Rin," Jim instructed. He and Mama advanced on Wesley shoulder to shoulder, equally grim looks on their faces.

"Good boy," Rin called obediently. "Come here now." The pup released Wesley and ran toward Rin. He skidded in the dirt as he came to a stop and panted happily up at Rin, who couldn't help reaching out to rub the pup's ears.

You have a name for him yet? Blue asked.

"I don't know. What's the Celtic word for 'white'?" Rin replied.

Boring. Think of something else.

"You've done enough tricking and stealing, Wesley," Mama was saying firmly across the yard. "You need to stop before you get in even more over your head."

Wesley opened and closed his mouth a few times. He was shaking all over, his eyes wide with shock, and he didn't seem to know which part of Jim's unglamored form to stare at first.

"I think the best thing for him is to erase his memory of the last few days," Jim said after studying Wesley for a moment. "Make him forget about magic and the fae, and even forget about his plans to steal our horses."

"Fine," Mama replied shortly. "Get on with it so we can get back to our chores." She glanced over her shoulder as she said that. While her glance was as assessing as it was pointed—she no doubt wanted to make sure for herself that Rin was okay—Rin got the message.

"Help me up," he told Blue, who scrambled to his feet before holding out his hands for Rin to take.

Rin felt fine. He should have felt wobbly or unsteady, but he felt as strong as he had before the fight. He checked Blue over quickly, too, while their hands were clasped, healing the few bruises and scratches Blue had gotten in the last part of the fight.

Jim's hands were glowing as he traced symbols in the air over Wesley's head, and he was mumbling something under his breath. Mama was looking at Rin, watching him stand and then walk into the barn without even a limp. Rin didn't doubt she was going to insist on him taking a hot bath later to soothe any remaining aches, which Rin didn't mind, since he was sure Blue would be happy to join him.

Inside the barn was still cool from the summer night. The heat of the day always took a while to penetrate the wide space. Rin welcomed the warmth, letting it finish steadying his frayed nerves. He was trying very hard not to think of that fight. Not being able to breathe was terrifying, but seeing Blue slumped on the ground had been even more so. If Rin allowed himself to dwell, he knew he would start shaking and crying again.

There was no reason to break down like that. They had won the fight, everyone was alive, and Rin had healed all of Blue's injuries. It was only a delayed reaction from the adrenaline, Rin tried to tell himself, hoping his nightmares wouldn't be too bad.

Demon's stall was halfway down the line, and Blue let out an unhappy whinny when they arrived.

Poor horsie! Blue gasped. He yanked open the stall door and hurried inside to Demon's side.

Demon's large body was pressed against the back wall of his stall, far away from what must have been terrible noise coming in from the barn's front door. He was shaking uncontrollably, the same way Rin was fighting to keep himself from doing. Blue whickered at Demon.

It's okay. It's all over. The scary bit is done.

Blue's words were for Demon, but they soothed Rin's fears too. He followed Blue into the stall and carefully patted Demon's neck.

"It's okay, Demon," Rin said, echoing Blue's words out loud. "It's over. I'm sorry you were scared by it. I think we all were."

Outside was the rumble of an engine starting and the faint crunch of tires turning out of the yard. Jim had finished with Wesley and was sending him away. It was over.

Mama came running into the barn. She stopped outside Demon's stall when she saw what Rin and Blue were doing.

"Rin, go make Demon a mash and grab some of the peppermints, see if that will help calm him down," Mama said.

Rin gave Demon's neck one last, gentle pat, before pulling away. When he got out of the stall, Mama grabbed him, pulling him tight in a hug. She didn't say anything, but the neck of his shirt dampened where her face was pressed. Mama pushed him away a few seconds later, and Rin walked away to where the feed was kept.

It took him a few minutes to mix the ingredients correctly in the big bucket they used for the horses. By the time he returned, Demon had stopped shaking, although he was still pressed against the back wall of his stall. The scent of the food had his ears pricking up, and his nose was pushing into the bucket before Rin could pour its contents into his feed trough.

"Good food, gentle care, and a clean stall. That's all horses need," Mama said thoughtfully as she looked at Demon. "This one's finally starting to come around, I hope." She smiled at Rin and Blue. "When he finishes, put him in the paddock so he can get some exercise. Jim and I are going to go up to the pasture to check on the other horses. I want you to take a long bath after Demon's settled, Rin." Mama was definitely getting predictable, Rin thought with an inner smirk. "Ease whatever aches you have left over. Let's get everyone back into shiny health before Miach arrives."

Mama looked at Rin and Blue one more time, as if she still needed to double-check they were okay, before turning on her heel and striding out of the barn.

Demon didn't take long to scarf down his treat. Blue went to get a halter, and he slipped it over Demon's head while Demon was happily crunching a peppermint. Rin walked with Blue and Demon outside because he couldn't quite make himself leave Blue's side just yet. Blue let Demon into the paddock, and they headed back to the barn to muck out Demon's stall.

Rin's puppy was snoozing in the middle of the yard, flopped on his belly and looking self-satisfied even in sleep.

"What if I named him 'Snow'?" Rin asked.

Still boring. Keep thinking.

Rin couldn't help laughing. "Okay, Blue, I'll keep working on it."

Work faster. It's almost bath time. Rin didn't need Blue's pointed wink to understand what Blue meant. He hurried his feet back into the barn for the thankless task of mucking out Demon's stall. With the promise of a bath afterward, Rin couldn't help grinning the entire way.

Epilogue

Miach, my father, only stayed three days.

Do you have any idea how weird it is to know I have a father? I mean, of course I have a father, but knowing that and actually meeting him are two different things. It's hard to wrap my mind around a concept I hadn't had to think about for my entire life thus far.

He was nice, which I hadn't expected. Dian Cecht was so damned scary, and I half thought Miach would be the same. Apparently, he's been traveling the human world for longer than Mama's mama has been alive—although I'm the only kid he's had during that time—so he's figured out how to tone down the scary.

Miach took some time to sit down with Mama to apologize for leaving her alone when she got pregnant, but since he hadn't known I existed until the anti-Nuada faction had let slip that they were planning to kidnap me, Mama completely understood.

He also sat down with me. Miach wanted to spend some time with me to get to know me, and to teach me more magic.

You're starting the story wrong!

Sorry, Blue. You're right. Let me try again.

Good.

My daddy really was a cowboy, exactly as Mama always said. He likes to travel, and he doesn't have a home or a car or anything. Instead he travels across the country with the cows being shipped from place to place for whatever reason. A lot of the time that means he's on a train or in the cab of an eighteen-wheeler, but every once in a while, someone wants to drive their cows somewhere the old-fashioned way. His favorite time is on a horse with a pair of dogs, circling a herd to keep it moving.

Since he started his work as a cowboy back in the days when horses and dogs were the only means of moving cattle until the trains slowly began to come to the rural cities in the Midwest, my dad knows what he's doing. He could definitely teach me a few tricks in the saddle if I were ever interested in riding any horse aside from Blue ever again. Which I'm not.

Glad to hear that. Now I don't have to go eating any horses that don't stay away from what's mine.

You eat any of Mama's horses and she'll skin you alive, Blue.

She'll understand when I explain why.

Can I get back to my story now? Thanks, Blue.

Anyway, Miach only stayed for three days. Late summer is prime work time for him, so he left for a job down in Texas. I know he'll be back, probably in the winter when there is little need for a wrangler. There's still so much about magic and about Underhill that he needs to teach me. My heritage and the magic that comes easiest to me is the healing, but apparently, there's so much more. I'm excited to learn it, although I don't really want to go back to Underhill. Blue says he doesn't want to go back either, that he's so much happier now, here, than he ever was anywhere else.

Trust me, I'm definitely blushing after writing that, Blue. You being happy with me is something I will always cherish, but it feels so weird to write it down, like putting it in the open like this will expose some inner secret part of me. I don't have any secrets from you, Blue, so I know I'm just being silly.

I love you too, my pretty, pretty snack.

*

The mare yanked her head up, pulling on the reins in Rin's hands. Rin knew better than to let go, especially while he was holding a yearling, but he couldn't help scanning the crowd again quickly instead of focusing his attention on Cobalt Queen.

There! Miach was standing on the patron side of the fence in the shade cast by a family's overhead tent, a pleased grin on his face as he watched Rin and Blue walk down the horse path together at Cobalt Queen's side. That must be why Rin's mind had wandered back to his first journal entry about his father from two years ago, but it was time to stay focused now.

The murmurs around him intensified as the patrons checked their racing books and saw Cobalt Queen's lineage. Her sire was Swearing a Blue Streak, aka Demon Blue, and her dam was Queen of Sheeba. Cobalt Queen had Triple Crown–level breeding. Now they needed to see if she could run, although Rin didn't have any doubts of that. Queen was going to go far, and at a pace other horses were going to struggle to keep up with.

Once she broke her maiden, which was today's race, Mama would be sure to enter Queen in the races that would get her ready for the Triple Crown and whatever other stakes races Queen could safely fit in her schedule. Since she was the first yearling to come out of Mama's renewed breeding program, Mama wanted to be careful, yet aggressive at the same time. It was going to be amazing to be a part of.

Queen can do this. If I can do this, Queen can do this. Right? Blue asked apprehensively.

Queen's head was high and her eyes were bright with intelligence as she looked at the patrons as she walked past them. Nothing spooked her. Rin stood proudly at her side, wearing the pink jersey that denoted he was her hot-walker. Blue walked with them, but Mama had chosen to wait for them in the paddock with Jim, whose glamor had been altered slightly so he wouldn't be recognized. Jim O'Malley and Overhill Stables were officially shut down until Mama was ready to finish training and racing horses and give them over to Jim.

They reached the paddock a minute later, and Rin brought Queen over to where Mama and Jim were waiting underneath the correct tree. The saddle came a few minutes later, quickly followed by the jockey.

"Riders up!"

Rin circled Queen one last time to check her stride before lining her up along the outer path of the paddock with the other yearlings in the race. Mama boosted the jockey into place on Queen's back, and then they walked on the path, out of the paddock and to the track where the jockey and an outrider took over from there.

"Let's go watch from next to the winner's circle," Rin called to his family. Blue slid his hand into Rin's and led the way with a happy whinny.

They managed to find a place along the fence and watched as Queen was loaded into the starting gate. Rin's back was pressed against Blue's chest, and Blue's warmth helped stifle the butterflies trying to flutter through Rin's stomach.

Queen's strong. Besides, you trained her, Rin. She'll be great. Blue nuzzled Rin's hair in comfort, and Rin let out a breath he hadn't realized he had been holding.

The bell rang, the gates popped open, and the announcer came over the speakers.

"And they're off!"

About the Author

When Mell Eight was in high school, she discovered dragons. Beautiful, wondrous creatures that took her on epic adventures both to faraway lands and on journeys of the heart. Mell wanted to create dragons of her own, so she put pen to paper. Mell Eight is now known for her own soaring dragons, as well as for other wonderful characters dancing across the pages of her books. While she mostly writes paranormal or fantasy stories, she has been seen exploring the real world once or twice.

Facebook
www.facebook.com/MellEightFiction

Twitter
@MellEight

Website
www.melleightfiction.weebly.com

Other NineStar books by this author

Ge-Mi, Part One

Ge-Mi, Part Two

Supernatural Consultant Series

Dragon Consultant

Dragon Deception

Dragon Dilemma

Dragon Detective

Dragon Soldier

Dragon Adventures

Dragon Lesson

Also from NineStar Press

Connect with NineStar Press

www.ninestarpress.com

www.facebook.com/ninestarpress

www.facebook.com/groups/NineStarNiche

www.twitter.com/ninestarpress